Shoebag

Shoebag

by Mary James

AN
APPLE
PAPERBACK

SCHOLASTIC INC.
New York Toronto London Auckland Sydney

Copyright © 1990 by Mary James.
All rights reserved. Published by Scholastic Inc.
Printed in the U.S.A.

ISBN 0-439-06408-2

SCHOLASTIC, APPLE PAPERBACKS, READ 180, and associated logos and designs are trademarks and/or registered trademarks of Scholastic Inc.
LEXILE is a trademark of MetaMetrics, Inc.

2   3   4   5   6   7   8   9   10   23   06   05   04   03   02   01

For James and Klarene Kamitses
of Sunnyvale, California,
with much love.

One

Like all cockroaches, Shoebag was named after his place of birth. He was snoozing there now, in the open toe of a white summer sandal. He was having his old dream of growing big enough to squash the seven-legged, black jumping spider and of moving somewhere warm and dark and filled with meats, cheeses, sweets, and starches.

All of Shoebag's family dreamed about living in a safer neighborhood, even though this building in Boston was home sweet home. Already they had lost two aunts and a cousin to the jumping spider, and one grandfather, plus several uncles to water bugs and beetles, wasps, centipedes, and the dread fumes of Zap.

Their apartment was fumigated on the first Monday of every month, when they had to scamper through underground passages to the building next door. There they waited until the dread fumes were gone. Then they went back.

Boston, Massachusetts, was known for its cold, cold winters. But even if the family was lucky enough one day to get a ride in a box going somewhere else, there was no assurance that they would be settled in a warmer climate. Neighbors they knew had escaped in a packing crate some time ago, only to find themselves in Bangor, Maine, where it was even colder.

"Wake up, Shoebag!" his mother shouted. "The jumping spider in the kitchen has let down his dragline! He'll be here soon!"

Of all their enemies, the black jumping spider was the fiercest, and almost as violent as his fat and hairy brown brother from next door.

Quick and tricky, he had no web. He let himself down from high levels on the dragline of silk he spun in his spinnerets.

"Death to all insects!" he called out, for like all spiders, he was not an insect but an arachnid. He had no jaws. He had many eyes. He would have had eight legs, as all arachnids do, except that a Persian cat from the third floor had pulled one off.

"Shoebag!" his mother's voice again, this time from the top of a Reebok next to the sandal, "Hurry up! Get your cerci moving!"

A cerci is what cockroaches call their tails.

Shoebag was anxious to get his cerci moving.

His mother's antennae made a light puff of air. A cerci is a remarkably sensitive structure, and even a light puff of air directed at a cerci sends a cockroach scurrying. But Shoebag did not move.

The trouble was, Shoebag couldn't get his cerci to go.

The reason was, Shoebag's cerci was missing.

So were his two back legs.

So were his two middle legs.

So were his two front legs.

And so were his antennae.

Something terrible had happened to Shoebag.

Shoebag's mother was named Drainboard. His father's name was Under The Toaster.

When Drainboard took a good look at Shoebag her wings fluttered down, her shell quivered, and she called out, "Under The Toaster, come here immediately! Something's happened to Shoebag!"

"Something terrible happened to me!" Shoebag said. "I am changed!"

"You certainly are changed!" said Drainboard.

Under The Toaster hopped out of a black loafer and stared with horror at his son. "You really are changed! Ugh! *Are* you!"

"I have tiny hands," Shoebag said. "I have tiny feet! I have a tiny nose and tiny ears! I have a tiny head!"

"With hair!" Under The Toaster exclaimed.

"You have eyebrows and eyelashes!" Drainboard groaned.

"You have a neck and a chest and a stomach," Under The Toaster complained.

3

"I have become a tiny person," said Shoebag.

"You have become quite repulsive!" Under The Toaster told the truth, and the truth made Shoebag's father shiver with disgust.

"I cannot stand myself! Yeck!" said Shoebag looking at his new body.

"Now you will get dirty the way people do." His mother was backing away from him.

"This is the worst thing that has ever happened to me." Shoebag was waving his new tiny hands, staring with awe at his new tiny fingers, then stamping his new tiny feet.

It was right at that moment that the black, seven-legged jumping spider swung down on his dragline from a wooden coat hanger above them.

"Whoops!" he said, when he saw Shoebag, for he had not counted on meeting up with a person. "My mistake!" and he tried getting back up to the closet shelf.

Shoebag picked the spider up and tossed him through the crack of the closet door.

"Go after him and pull off his other legs!" Drainboard said.

"I am not that much of a person," Shoebag protested. "I can't pull legs off."

"Then step on him!" Under The Toaster yelled.

"I have no shoes on," Shoebag said. "I cannot step on something that will squish in my bare feet!"

Shoebag could not believe that he had actually

touched an arachnid, and the black jumping spider at that!

"You cannot run around naked, either, now that you are a tiny person," said Drainboard, philosophically.

"I'll need tiny clothes," Shoebag said.

"You'll need light," Under The Toaster said.

"I'll need money," Shoebag said. "I'll need toys. I'll need candy. I'm a tiny person."

"You'll need three meals a day," Drainboard said. "Our picnics won't be enough for you."

"You won't be satisfied with other people's crumbs," said Under The Toaster.

"You'll need soap and a washcloth," said Drainboard. "You'll need a bed and sheets and blankets and a pillow."

"I'll need television," said Shoebag. "I'm a tiny person!"

"We can't give you any of those things," said Drainboard.

"We will probably have to disown you now," said Under The Toaster.

"You are my family, though," said Shoebag. "You are the only family I have."

"You will have to go someplace and forget all about us," said Under The Toaster.

"Go where? Where will I go?"

"Someplace you can't step on us," said Drainboard. "You are a person now, and you will want to step on us."

"I will never be that big a person," Shoebag said. "I will never want to step on my own mother and father."

"You are too big already!" Drainboard said. "If you wanted to get back inside your shoebag, you couldn't do it anymore. You can't crawl through the cracks, or hide behind doorknobs, or skitter up lamp cords, or anything!"

This was true. Shoebag had grown larger than he'd ever dreamed he could be, even though he was just a little boy.

"I am getting scared of you," said Under The Toaster. "You may be my own son, but you no longer resemble me."

"I am getting scared of myself," said Shoebag. "This is no time to abandon me. Now more than ever I need you."

"Before you grow another inch," Drainboard said, "promise you'll never step on your own mother."

"He can't keep promises," said Under The Toaster. "He's a person."

"I'm only a little person, so I can keep little promises," said Shoebag.

"A promise not to step on us is not such a little promise," said Drainboard. "It's a big promise."

"I can handle it," Shoebag told her.

"You don't know that," said Under The Toaster. "You don't know the things people are capable of doing."

6

"I know that now I'm one of them, and I know that I will never step on my own parents."

"People do things and say the things they did were accidents," said Under The Toaster.

"I will be very, very careful!" Shoebag vowed. "Do you think I want to be an orphan?"

"Whisper!" said Under The Toaster. "Your voice hurts my ears."

Shoebag whispered, "I will never harm you, and I will be very, very careful." Then Shoebag had the first happy thought since he had become this little person. He began to whisper harder. "When I get shoes I will crush the seven-legged, black jumping spider," he said, "and his fat, hairy brown brother from next door! And when I get clothes with pockets I will collect little picnics and bring them to you."

"The air from your whisper hurts my antennae," said Drainboard.

"And it is too hot," said Under The Toaster. "You are talking hot air!"

Shoebag covered his mouth with his new hand. "Is that better?"

"A little, but don't move your foot until I get up on the wall. You almost broke your promise to us."

"I can't see in here, that's why," said Shoebag. "Let me reach up and turn on the light."

"No, not that bright light!" said Drainboard. "Please!"

7

"But how can I see you?"

"We'll tell you when we're safely out of sight," said Under The Toaster.

Shoebag waited in the dark. He had always liked the dark, always run to dark places, but now he found that he was afraid of the dark.

Anything could happen in the dark to a person. He had seen that with his own eyes. He had seen people stumble and fall in the dark. He had seen people get mugged in the dark. He had always known that the first thing a person did when they entered a dark place was to turn on a light.

I don't think this is right, he told himself, that I should be standing here without any clothes on in a dark closet. I am just a little boy.

"Did you hear what I said?" Shoebag called out.

There was no answer.

Perhaps he had not said it aloud, for he was not yet used to being a person with this little voice.

"Where are you?" he called out. "Can you hear me?"

"I'm in the pocket of the . . ." and the rest of what Drainboard said was muffled.

"*Where?*" Shoebag said.

"Shhhhh!" from far away, from under wool or behind zippers, or inside coat linings, "Our ears! Hush!"

"WHERE ARE YOU?" Shoebag began to panic. "WHAT POCKET?"

He stood in the dark listening.

When there was no answer, he felt so alone and desperate that he began to holler louder. "I'LL GO THROUGH ALL THESE POCKETS!"

"Oh, no, you won't!" a new voice, very much like his own, said. "Thief! Thief! Closet thief! Call the police!"

Two

Of course she heard all the racket going on downstairs in the hall, but Pretty Soft Biddle did not get involved in trouble.

She did not get involved in anything that might cause her to worry and frown, for that could make wrinkles someday on her face, and then where would she be?

"Thief! Thief! Closet thief!"

Pretty Soft reached for the television remote control and pushed Volume Up.

It was almost time for her commercial, too, and even though she had played it over and over on the VCR, she liked to see it afternoons when it came on in the middle of soaps. She liked to hear it at full volume.

Her real name was Eunice Biddle, but everyone called her Pretty Soft. Her father did. Her mother did. The Postman did. Her relatives did. Her tutor and manager, Madam Grande de la Grande did, and her fans certainly did.

She was seven years old, but she still looked about four. It was her dearest wish that she would look four forever, though she knew it was probably not a wish that could come true.

Pretty Soft could still hear some noise from downstairs, and she was afraid that if it did not stop, she would wonder about it. If she wondered too hard about it, next thing she knew she might wrinkle her brow, a thing she would never do if she could help it.

So she put down the television remote and picked up one of her mirrors. The white one which went with the white furniture, the white rug, and the white drapes in the living room where she was sitting.

She stared into this mirror which was always in the living room, and she said what she always said to her reflection when she could feel herself about to get tense.

Pretty Soft said, "I see my own beauty, may it last forever."

"WHAT KIND OF A NAME IS THAT, YOUNG MAN?" her father was downstairs shouting. "TELL ME YOUR REAL NAME IMMEDIATELY!"

Then, as though The Fates were sparing her anymore unnecessary intrusion, Pretty Soft's music began playing from the television.

She put down the mirror.

She fluffed out her long blonde hair, leaned back against the soft white couch cushions, crossed her legs, and folded her arms, hugging herself. Her light blue eyes twinkled, and her dimples showed, and even though it was a sign of vanity to feel such joy when she saw herself on television, Pretty Soft could not stop the little smile of pleasure that always came to her mouth.

Now the chorus of toilet paper rolls was dancing merrily down the green hill, unfurling amid buttercups and brown-eyed Susans, as they sang:

> *Six hundred sheets a roll, and soft as any*
> *kitty,*
> *We're double-layered, too, and people say*
> *we're pretty,*
> *We come in shades of blue and beige, green,*
> *yellow, and pure white,*
> *We think you'll like our talcumed scent and*
> *say we're bathroom right.*

A close-up as Pretty Soft spoke, holding a Persian cat to her face, "If you have Pretty Soft in your bathroom, your guests will purrrrrr!"

(Mildred, the cat, never purred, though. She hated being on television, where they did not even call her by her own name.)

Fade out as Pretty Soft said, "Won't they, Whiskers?"

And the announcer's voice cooed, "You bet they will, Pretty Soft!"

Pretty Soft never played with other boys and girls. Her manager and tutor, Madam Grande de la Grande, called them civilians, which was her name for all ordinary people who were not stars.

"Civilians," said Madam G. de la G., "will always be jealous of you, and they will be the first to turn against you. Stay out of their way, child."

"But what about my own parents? Aren't they civilians?"

"They are, but they are your parents, so it is all right."

"And what about *you*, Madam Grande de la Grande?"

"Ah, but I was a star once myself! Gloria Grande de la Grande, known far and wide as Glorious Gloria. My name was on every lip!"

Pretty Soft had asked her, "Then what happened?"

"I had no one to tell me how to prevent wrinkles and lines, so one day my poor face was full of them! I was forced to switch from performing to managing and tutoring."

"And you found me," Pretty Soft had said happily.

"Exactly, Precious, but don't smile so widely. A wide smile leaves marks, child. Keep your joy inside or you'll ruin the outside."

Madam Grande de la Grande always wore a long black cape, a velvet one in winter and a silk one in summer, for she was in mourning for her dead career. But around her neck there was a fire-colored scarf, to match her hair, and to represent the flame of talent, so she said, the new, hot promise of someone like Pretty Soft.

It was she who had taught Pretty Soft what to say to her mirror. It was she who had instructed Pretty Soft to always have one nearby.

"A mirror will tell you what you are and who you are and how you are and why you are."

"And where I am?" Pretty Soft had asked.

"Yes, that, too, if you stand back far enough."

Pretty Soft turned down the volume of the television and listened.

Everything was so quiet suddenly.

Probably her father had taken the closet thief to the police . . . and probably her mother was in the kitchen preparing dinner.

Every night at this time, an hour before the family sat down in the dining room, Pretty Soft read something beautiful and inspiring, so that when she ate her food, it would be properly digested, because her mind was free of all but lovely thoughts.

" 'Beauty is like the surf that never ceases,' " Pretty Soft read from the writings of Struthers Burt. " 'Beauty is like the night that never dies. Beauty is like a forest pool where . . .' "

"Hello? Hello?" a voice called from the hall. "Pretty Soft? Are you up here?"

"Who is calling me?" said Pretty Soft, who knew every voice that ever said her name in this house, but did not know this one.

"Your father sent me up to be with you," the voice answered. "My name is Shoebag. Don't laugh."

Pretty Soft couldn't help it. She laughed that lilting way the television people always said she should as she looked down at Whiskers at the end of the commercial. This time it was not forced, and she had not had to do a dozen retakes: It just flowed forth from her insides. For what kind of a name was Shoebag? What kind of a person had a name like that?

She soon discovered that the kind of person who had a name like Shoebag was a small, red-headed boy with blue eyes and freckles, barefoot, and wrapped in a blanket.

He was standing in the doorway.

"I knew you'd laugh. I told your father you would and you did."

"I didn't want to laugh," Pretty Soft told him. "I'll get laugh lines, if I laugh that way very often, so I save such a laugh for when I work. But Shoebag is a funny name!"

"So I'm told," the little boy said.

"What happened to your clothes, Shoebag? Did the closet thief steal them?"

15

"May I come in and sit down before I answer any more questions?" he asked her. "Your father has gone to get me something to wear."

"Come in, then," Pretty Soft said.

And so it was, that on the third of March, in Boston, Massachusetts, Shoebag entered the life of Eunice Biddle, also known as Pretty Soft, and neither of them would ever be the same again.

Three

Now this is what we are going to do!" said Mr. Biddle, who was a store manager, good at making decisions and seeing to it that they were put into action. "First, we are going to give Shoebag a proper name."

"I won't remember to answer to a new name," said Shoebag. "I have been called Shoebag all my life."

"You'll remember it if it's close to Shoebag," said Mr. Biddle. "When you first said your name, I thought you said Stu Bag, so that's what we'll call you, hmmm? Stuart Bag."

"Stu Bag," said Pretty Soft. "Who could forget a name like that?"

"It doesn't make any sense," said Shoebag. "What is a stu bag? It sounds like a bag full of stew."

"If there's an extra g on Bag, it will look better," said Mrs. Biddle, who was an artist, and very concerned with how things looked. "Stuart *B a g g*. That's a very decent name."

"But what does it even *mean?*" said Shoebag.

"It means it's your name." Mr. Biddle was a no-nonsense type who had a black mustache he kept clean with a special little comb.

The Biddles and Shoebag were sitting around the table in the dining room. They had just finished a dinner of spaghetti, which looked to Shoebag like a plate of worms, so he'd enjoyed it, although he'd never eaten a worm, not even on a rainy day, when he'd hopped over them outdoors on the sidewalk.

"Worms have no backbone!" Drainboard used to comment. "And I have no use for them."

Shoebag had a strong suspicion the Biddle family would have no use for him, if he were to tell them he was once a cockroach, so he kept quiet about it.

He remembered what Under The Toaster used to say. "When the lights are out, we're all one big happy family in this apartment building, but as soon as they go on, we're the enemy!"

"Why?" Shoebag would ask him.

"Because people just don't take to us. I think it's our looks or something."

"It *is* our looks," said Drainboard. "And this will give you a laugh, Son, *they* think *we're* dirty!"

"That doesn't give me a laugh," Shoebag had answered. "It makes me sad, instead. After all, it's their dirt we drag around on our feet."

"Tell *them* that," Drainboard had said. "They

18

think that with all the baths and showers they take, with all the deodorants and mouthwash and perfume they use, they're clean!"

"A person never stays clean, though," Under The Toaster had remarked in his most discouraged tone. "There's just too much to keep clean on a person."

Shoebag knew the truth of that now. He'd no sooner stepped out of the shower than his toes had picked up lint from the bathroom rug, and next his hands had gotten dusty from the staircase railing. His teeth had spaghetti sauce in the crevices right this minute, and there was a milk stain already on the new blue shirt Mr. Biddle had bought for him.

"The next thing we have to do is enroll Stu in the Beacon Hill Elementary School," said Mr. Biddle, "unless of course you're a Catholic? Are you a Catholic?"

Shoebag said what he always said when he was asked a personal question. "I can't remember anything but my name."

"Oh, dear, oh, dear, you really do have amnesia," said Mrs. Biddle, the only one still eating, the only plump Biddle.

"What is amnesia?" Pretty Soft asked.

Mr. Biddle let out a huge sigh which made his mustache wiggle, and he rolled his eyes up toward the ceiling. "You don't know what amnesia is? You're seven years old and you don't know that amnesia means a memory loss?"

"How would I know that?" said Pretty Soft.

"We are paying Madam Grande de la Grande your hard-earned money to teach you things like that," said Mr. Biddle.

"How do you lose your memory?" Pretty Soft asked.

"We don't have all the answers on that one," her father told her, "but sometimes it happens if you hit your head on something hard, and sometimes a person is in a bad accident and he comes out unable to say who he is or where he lives. And often . . ."

Pretty Soft began to hold up her hands and make a face. "Please! Stop! Do not tell me about bad things! I will only go to sleep and have a nightmare about not being able to remember my lines! You are not supposed to put ugly thoughts in my head, Daddy!"

Mrs. Biddle said, "Pretty Soft is right."

"The child is living in a dream world," Mr. Biddle grumbled.

"But that dream world will one day pay for her college education," said his wife. "Let's remember that."

Shoebag spoke up then. He had been sitting there between Pretty Soft's parents trying to imagine himself attending Beacon Hill Elementary School. The more he'd thought about it, the more he'd hated the idea of being thrown in with other boys and girls who'd had more practice being people than he could ever hope to have.

What would become of him in such a place?

Wasn't it likely that he'd be slower than the others, and that he'd seem strange and out-of-place there? Wouldn't they pick on him, call him names, humiliate him, push him, even knock him down in the recess yard?

"Why do I have to go to school?" he asked Mr. Biddle, who seemed to be in charge. "Why can't I be tutored as Pretty Soft is?"

"You can't afford it," Pretty Soft said. "You don't have any money, *do* you?"

"Darling, he can't remember anything," said Mrs. Biddle.

"He doesn't look like someone with money," Pretty Soft said. "He didn't even have clothes. He was trying to steal ours from the closet!"

"I was *not!*" said Shoebag.

"Well, you were going through our pockets!" said Pretty Soft, who seemed to Shoebag to be neither pretty nor soft when it came to money.

"Hush! Hush! Hush!" Mr. Biddle said. "We have a lot to settle tonight, and I have bills to send out. . . . Pretty Soft, you must learn to be more kind to Stuart Bagg, since we have taken him under our roof."

Shoebag felt very much like announcing that it was more his roof than their roof, since his family and his ancestors had been in this old apartment building for generations. But he was in no position to throw his new little human weight around.

Mr. Biddle said, "And Shoebag, tomorrow morning at seven-thirty, you and I will stroll down to Beacon Hill Elementary School, where I will introduce you to the principal before I go to my store."

"Who are you going to say he is?" asked Mrs. Biddle. "I know you're going to say his name is Stuart Bagg, but what relationship will you say we have with him?"

"I'll say he is our new adopted boy," said Mr. Biddle.

"You always wanted a son." Mrs. Biddle smiled.

"And I always wanted a brother!" said Pretty Soft.

"So everyone is happy," Mr. Biddle said.

"But tell him, Daddy. Be sure he knows the rule."

"He has to know the rule," Mrs. Biddle agreed.

"Stu, *Son*," said Mr. Biddle, "as a rule, we don't discuss bad things in front of Pretty Soft. It is very important to always emphasize the positive where she's concerned.

"And eliminate the negative," said Pretty Soft.

"But what do you do when bad things happen?" Shoebag asked. "What do you do if the wind breaks the windows, or the rain comes in, or thunder shakes the whole house with a terrible boom?"

"We tend to it without disturbing Pretty Soft," said Mr. Biddle. "It is very dangerous to her career if she becomes upset, you see."

"And I know how to deal with anything that might threaten me," said Pretty Soft. "Come over here, and I'll show you how I do it."

Shoebag climbed down from his chair and went around to hers.

"Here by my plate I always keep the dining room mirror, which is yellow, because the dining room is yellow," said Pretty Soft. "Then I look into it, and this is what I say."

Shoebag looked into the mirror with her.

"I say, 'I see my own beauty, may it last forever.' "

"That's what she says," Mrs. Biddle said.

"That's what she always says, and it seems to work," Mr. Biddle said.

To Shoebag's horror, as he looked into the mirror with Pretty Soft, he saw a lovely little blonde face on the right, and on the left, he saw himself, his true self: a cockroach with its antennae trembling.

"Aren't we cute together?" Pretty Soft smiled in the reflection, while Shoebag's brown shell shuddered.

"We are like brother and sister," said Pretty Soft.

"Do you like the way I look?" Shoebag asked.

"Of course I do!" she replied . . . and it was then that Shoebag realized she did not see what he saw in that mirror.

"Of course she does!" said Mrs. Biddle.

"Why wouldn't she?" Mr. Biddle said. "You are a very, very nice-looking young fellow."

"Thank you," came from the cockroach mouth, and Shoebag's wings lifted and fell in the old roach signal of contentment.

23

Four

For an hour before bedtime, Shoebag was invited to watch television with Pretty Soft, in her all-pink room.

Pretty Soft always watched her two favorite sitcoms then, each one a half hour long.

Shoebag was not a regular television viewer, since he and his family always foraged for food in people's kitchens when they turned on their sets.

He leaned back on Pretty Soft's pink velvet chaise and laughed and laughed at all the jokes, but Pretty Soft kept a straight face. She was lathering it with Chase Away, an anti-wrinkle cream. She was propped up against the pink pillows on her bed. She wore a pink kimono, and pink scuffs, and kept her pink mirror beside her.

Shoebag waited until a commercial for hair spray came on, before he asked her why she watched this sitcom called "Molly Moon," if she didn't think it was funny.

"I think it's hilarious," she told him, "and one of the reasons I watch it, is because it has a laugh track."

Shoebag didn't know what that meant.

"Wherever you came from," she said, "it couldn't have been a very civilized place, or you would know more about television. All that laughter you hear is pre-recorded, what we call canned laughter. The television producers stick it in after someone does or says something funny. That's why I don't laugh. They do the laughing for me."

"But I can't *help* laughing," said Shoebag.

"Then laugh. Most home viewers do, but I have to save my face."

"If most home viewers laugh, why is there a laugh track then?"

"Because some people don't get the jokes," Pretty Soft said, "and because some people don't like to laugh alone. They feel like they're having a better time if everyone is laughing."

Now Pretty Soft had put down Chase Away to brush her hair, 100 strokes in front, 100 strokes in back, and 100 strokes on both sides. She was counting under her breath.

Suddenly there was a familiar sight on the big 25 inch screen. Cockroaches. Dozens of them running around a giant chunk of Swiss cheese.

Shoebag felt a thrill of recognition. Here were his own kind on television! If there were cockroaches featured on prime time on national TV, they could not be as hated as his family had always claimed. Shoebag felt proud, and he looked across at Pretty Soft to see her reaction.

". . . twenty-nine, thirty, thirty-one," she was counting as she combed her hair, and although her eyes were on the screen, Shoebag could tell nothing about her feelings.

He was planning to exclaim on cockroach bravery (risking exposure and eye glare under those bright television lights) and their great beauty (they had chosen only the ones with the shiniest shells and the longest antennae). But something catastrophic happened before Shoebag could speak.

A great white cloud was puffed at the cockroaches causing them to fall over, legs up, as it mushroomed over their little bodies and hung above them.

An announcer's voice with a particularly ominous tone, said "Zap zaps cockroaches dead!"

"Oh, no," said Shoebag. "Zap!"

"It's awfully smelly stuff, isn't it?" Pretty Soft commented. "On the first Monday of every month, when they fumigate here, I go to the park with Madam G. de la G. Then mother sprays the house with Fresh Meadow Scent, so there's no foul odors left when I get back."

There was not one survivor on the TV screen . . . and now a large hand with wrist hairs was holding up a can of Zap.

"Zap!" said the announcer's voice. "For things that don't deserve to live!"

Shoebag said, "Why don't they?"

The announcer couldn't answer Shoebag, of course, but Pretty Soft did as she ran the pink hairbrush through the left side of her long blonde hair ". . . sixty . . . sixty-one, sixty-two . . . because they're ugly little insects," she said. "And they're filthy!"

"They've been around for 250 million years," Shoebag said. "They were here 249 million years before you were!"

"I don't care what was here before I was," said Pretty Soft.

"They don't harm people."

"They hide out in drainboards, under toasters, anywhere they feel like it, in people's homes."

"They were here first!" Shoebag said. "People moved into *their* homes."

"But cockroaches don't have leases," said Pretty Soft. "People have leases. We have a three-year lease on this apartment, and we'll probably renew it."

"A lease is just a piece of paper!" said Shoebag.

"But if you don't have one," Pretty Soft said, "you can't live in an apartment . . . unless of course you buy the building. I very much doubt that cockroaches make any money."

"Is money all you care about?" Shoebag asked. He was still badly shaken by the sight of his own species flat on their backs, feet-up, dead.

"I care about being beautiful first," said Pretty Soft, "because if I wasn't beautiful I wouldn't have so much money."

"Aren't there other ways to make money?" Shoebag asked.

"Not when you're only seven years old," Pretty Soft said. "Wherever you came from, you have forgotten how hard life really is sometimes."

No, Shoebag had not forgotten that at all, but he was surprised to hear Pretty Soft say such a thing.

"*You* think life is hard?" he asked her.

"I protect myself against it all the time," she told him. "I shouldn't even be having this conversation, for example."

"Why not?" Shoebag asked.

"Because I have already lost count of my brushstrokes," Pretty Soft said. "I have already broken my routine. It's not good to break your routine, not when it interferes with the business at hand."

With that, she began all over again on the left side of her head, counting, "One, two, three . . ."

Shoebag turned his attention back to the sitcom, but not before saying The Cockroach Prayer for the Dead.

"Go to a better life. Amen."

Five

The Biddle apartment was composed of the first two floors of the old brownstone. For all of their lives, Shoebag's family had lived on the bottom floor, where the kitchen, dining room, and Mrs. Biddle's studio was. They stayed mainly in the kitchen, behind things, but Shoebag had often played in the studio, where there were always cans of paint in many colors, and great canvases with paintings of the sea on them.

Shoebag had never seen a real sea with waves and sand and a beach. But sometimes he would run up and down one of the pictures, trying to imagine his legs getting wet as they left the tan colors and headed for the gray-green of the ocean, trying to feel the wind as he scampered higher into the blue, resting, out of breath, on one of the white clouds.

Mrs. Biddle had just finished making herself a salami sandwich on rye and carried it into the studio, where she was watching the ten o'clock news.

Shoebag had sneaked down the stairs in his new blue-and-white striped pajamas, with the white terrycloth robe. In his hurry to buy Shoebag clothes quickly, before dinner, Mr. Biddle had forgotten bedroom slippers, so Shoebag wore only socks. He could feel the cold of the linoleum floors right through the cotton. Skin was hard to keep warm, Shoebag realized. He missed the protection of his shell, but that was the least of it when it came to missing things.

He missed the freedom he had had to roam about at night. Mr. Biddle had made a bed for him on the couch, upstairs in the living room. He had told him lights out by ten P.M., which meant Shoebag was expected to go to sleep at that hour!

Shoebag also missed the old roach thrill at the approach of the nightly hunt for food. He knew that in back of the stove, under the refrigerator, behind the cupboard, and down near the dishwasher, all his family was gathered with their antennae alert, waiting for the house to settle down, their hopes rising as they speculated over what would be waiting for them, starting with the goodies usually found in the kitchen. (Already Shoebag could see all the bread crumbs on the counter, left by Mrs. Biddle, and the salami grease still streaked across the carving knife.)

Most of all, though, Shoebag missed Drainboard.

He worried that Under The Toaster would do what he had always done: run out ahead of her and

30

grab all the best food for himself. Shoebag had been faster than his father, and his eyesight had been better, so that when he was still one of the family, he jumped on choice morsels and saved them for his mother.

Under The Toaster claimed that the father cockroach came first, because after all he had to shoulder all the responsibility for the family. It was he who had to keep track of when the Zap man came, and it was he who had to decide if they should take a chance and move to a new place when a person packed up anything to be sent somewhere. (Never mind that Under The Toaster probably could not bring himself to leave Boston, or even this brownstone on Beacon Hill, because Shoebag's father, at heart, was very sentimental about both places.)

Under The Toaster was also supposed to be the lookout for the water bugs, the black jumping spider, and the ones in webs, the Persian cat from the third floor who often got loose, and any other enemies. Still, it was Drainboard who excelled at sensing danger. It was her voice most often calling out, "Get your cerci moving! Trouble is coming!"

As much as Shoebag honored Under The Toaster, he was his father, after all, he sometimes felt his mother was taken advantage of. Under The Toaster took the warmest sleeping place for himself. And he was always criticizing Drainboard for things like not warning him the dishwasher had not completed its cycle, so it would start up again, just as Under

The Toaster had crawled behind it. Or he would shout at Drainboard that she should have told him there was a roast in the oven, and not let him find it out for himself as he hopped down to the hot burner.

So Shoebag was filled with concern for Drainboard, which was why he had sneaked down to the first floor, past his bedtime.

He could hear the television weatherman from inside Mrs. Biddle's studio, forecasting snow.

Mrs. Biddle had left the little light on over the stove, and Shoebag climbed up on the kitchen stool and snapped it off.

"Mama?" he whispered. "Mama, it's me, your little boy, are you there?"

"Don't say that, honey, please," he heard her voice from somewhere. "It is bad enough what has happened to you, but call yourself my little son, not my little boy. Little boys kill roaches."

"I promised I wouldn't, Mama, and I won't. Are you all right?"

"I am, but your poor father is feeling badly. Look around and see if there's a choice morsel for him."

"There's salami grease on the knife, Mama, but I was hoping you'd have it."

"Would you put the knife up on the spice shelf for a moment? Your father is sleeping behind the cloves."

"What's wrong with him?" Shoebag asked as he

32

snapped on the stove light, got the knife from the counter, and opened the cupboard.

"He caught his left antenna in the oven door yesterday," said Drainboard. "It hurts him badly. He can't forage for food, or be the lookout, or any of that."

"Are you sure he isn't faking? He's done that before so that you end up doing all the work."

"SHUT THAT DOOR UNTIL YOU TURN OFF THE LIGHT!"

Shoebag turned off the light and stood in the dark on the stool. He was still very much afraid of his father's bad temper. Shoebag had not changed that much.

"There's salami grease on that knife, dear," said Drainboard to Under The Toaster.

"Don't you think I can see that? Do you think I'm blind?"

"Mama?" Shoebag said. "There are rye bread crumbs out here. Your favorite kind. Come out and get them."

"Thank heavens for Mrs. Biddle's gigantic appetite!" said Drainboard.

"Rye bread crumbs go with salami," said Under The Toaster. "Get *me* those rye bread crumbs!"

"They're for Mama," Shoebag said.

"Let Daddy have them," said Drainboard. "I'll come out later and look around for something."

"You could share them, there's plenty," said Shoebag.

"I need them all," said Under The Toaster. "I have an injured antenna, and I need to build up my strength."

"Get them for Daddy, dear. Make sure his door is shut, turn on the light, gather them up, turn the light off, open the door, and put them beside the knife."

Shoebag did all that, saying, "What about you, Mama?"

"Don't be such a mama's roach," snapped Under The Toaster. "I thought you were a person now."

"She's still my mother!" Shoebag said.

"And I'm still your father!" said Under The Toaster. "Show some respect. I eat first and best. I deserve special attention, too, now that I have injured my antenna. . . . Get this knife away, or someone will come along and suspect I'm behind the cloves!"

"Yes, sir!" said Shoebag, and he did as he was told.

"Don't worry about me, Shoebag," said his mother. "I'm not hungry now. I'll eat later."

That was what she always said.

"These rye bread crumbs are too fresh," said Under The Toaster. "I like them a little crustier."

"Then let Mama have them."

"I just ate the last one," said Under The Toaster with his mouth full. "Now see if you can find me something sweet for dessert."

"Is everything all right, my son?" Drainboard asked.

"Find me some cake," said Under The Toaster. "I feel like cake."

"Are you happy, Son?" said Drainboard.

"Let him find me some cake before you start all that questioning," Under The Toaster said.

"Don't you care how our little son is doing?" she asked him.

"I did, when he looked like me . . . but now . . ."

"Now what?" Shoebag asked him.

"Now get me some cake!" said Under The Toaster, and that was the point when Mrs. Biddle called out, "Who's in the kitchen? Rodney, is that you?"

Shoebag would have run back upstairs fast, except for what he saw crawling across the kitchen counter.

It was the seven-legged, black jumping spider.

Six

So it's you, Stu!" said Mrs. Biddle. "You should be asleep by now."

"I know it," Shoebag told her, "but I've been chasing a spider that I wish someone would kill."

Shoebag was still not sure he was enough of a person yet to kill the spider, and he did not have shoes on, either, to step on it.

Mrs. Biddle carried her plate to the kitchen counter. There were crusts of rye bread left on it, which Shoebag hoped she would forget to put into the garbage pail. It was not impossible for his family to get into the pail, but it was hard work, and Drainboard would be the one who would have to squeeze under the lid.

"Is it that spider over there?" Mrs. Biddle asked Shoebag as the jumping spider disappeared down the side of the stove.

"That's the one!" said Shoebag. "Get him while he's still around!"

"Darling, I never kill spiders. They're sweet little things, that one with the leg missing, in particular. . . . I feel sorry for him. I'd like to draw him someday."

"Then you're not afraid of spiders?"

Mrs. Biddle laughed. "Of course not! He's harmless."

"Do you kill other things?" Shoebag asked her.

"I don't like killing anything," said Mrs. Biddle. "I believe you live and let live."

"Do you kill cockroaches?"

Mrs. Biddle made a face. "Ugh! Yes! I kill them, because they are vermin. They are different."

"Why are they so different?"

"The way they look, for one thing. They are disgusting! And they are filthy, too!"

"But what about live and let live?"

"That's just an expression," said Mrs. Biddle. She reached for Shoebag's hand. "We don't care about cockroaches, honey, and you shouldn't be thinking about them late at night, or they'll get into your dreams. I'll walk you to the stairs. I still have work to do in my studio."

Then she called up the staircase, "Rodney? Tuck Stu in, darling! He's on his way up."

Mr. Biddle was sitting at his desk, in the little alcove around the corner from the living room.

"I thought you were asleep," he said.

Shoebag held out the hope that Mr. Biddle might feel differently about spiders, so he told him that

37

he was chasing one, which was still downstairs in the kitchen.

"The Zap man will be here tomorrow," Mr. Biddle said, "so don't worry." Mr. Biddle had his little comb out and was running it through his mustache. In front of him on his desk was a pen and what looked like a notebook.

"Are you sending your customers bills?" Shoebag asked.

"I'm finishing doing that. Now I'm about to write in my journal. You know, Son, it would be good for you to keep a journal. If you'd kept a journal before you lost your memory, all you would have to do is find it, and you would learn all about yourself and your other life."

"Does Pretty Soft keep a journal?"

"She keeps a diary she writes in, yes. I gave her one for Christmas."

"What does she write about?"

"Oh, we never read other people's journals or diaries, Son. They're private. You write down your most secret thoughts, and things that happened to you that are important. Tonight I'm going to write about you, and how you came into our life."

"I don't have a journal, though," said Shoebag.

"You can use an empty notebook I have here in my drawer," Mr. Biddle said. "And I'll get you a Flair pen to write with."

Mr. Biddle pulled open his desk drawer and got out the notebook and pen. Then he pushed back his chair. "I'll tuck you in now, and you can leave the light over the couch on for five minutes while you make your first entry in your new journal. How does that sound?"

"Good!" said Shoebag. "Are you sure no one will read it?"

"I promise you," Mr. Biddle said as they walked into the living room and over to the couch, which was made up like a bed.

When Shoebag was under the covers, Mr. Biddle leaned down and gave him a kiss on the forehead. His mustache tickled, but Shoebag liked it because it was his very first kiss from another person.

"Lights out in five minutes," said Mr. Biddle.

"Do I *have* to go to school tomorrow?" Shoebag asked him.

"You're not worried about that, are you? A big boy like you?"

"No," Shoebag lied, because he supposed big boys didn't worry about such things, and he did not want to give himself away.

"Good night," Mr. Biddle said. "Sleep tight, and don't let the bedbugs bite."

"Bedbugs?" Shoebag said. "Are there bedbugs in this couch?"

"That's just an expression, Son," said Mr. Biddle. "My heavens, where could you have come from that you've never heard that expression?"

Shoebag said, "Would you kill a bedbug if there was one in this couch?"

"You bet I would! But stop worrying about spiders and bugs and all those crawling critters. . . . Maybe in your other life you lived in some old, infested tenement, but now you're in a nice, clean, new home."

Shoebag was staring at the cotton socks he'd just removed and left on the floor. The bottoms were filthy from walking around on the Biddles' floors.

One thing that I have learned about people, Shoebag wrote in his first journal entry, *is that they don't think their own dirt is dirty. . . . They do not always mean the things they say, either, like live and let live . . . like good night, sleep tight, don't let the bedbugs bite. . . . Those are just expressions. . . . I miss my home sweet home!*

Now that I am a person, I do not always mean the things I say, either. I AM afraid to go to school tomorrow!

Shoebag was too worried to sleep, of course. It was twenty minutes to eleven when he put out the living room light, almost time for the late night picnic.

There was a moon shining into the living room, and Shoebag could see very well.

He waited for Mr. and Mrs. Biddle to go into their bedroom, waited until he could no longer see the crack of light under their door.

40

Then he sneaked back down the stairs and went into the kitchen.

There were no windows shining moonlight in there, so he had to feel his way around.

"Mama?" he called out. "It's me again!"

"I see you," she answered.

"Where are you?"

"Over here on the bread crusts. . . . Son, you have got to leave us alone. You're interfering with the late night picnic! Your aunts and uncles will be afraid to scavenge."

"But earlier I saw the black jumping spider in here!"

"He's next door visiting his fat, hairy brown brother now, Shoebag. Your father is watching for him. After your father ate, he felt much better."

"And tomorrow is the day the Zap man comes!"

"We know that. We plan to evacuate, as usual."

"Mama, I'm afraid to go to school."

"Don't shout, Son. Since you have become a little person, you are very noisy."

"I didn't think I was shouting," Shoebag whispered. "Did you hear what I said about school? I have to go to school tomorrow and I'm very afraid."

"Do you want me to go with you? Would that help?"

"Oh, Mama, yes! I will carry you with me in my pocket!"

"But just this once, honey. Mama can't always

be going places with you. Your father needs me, remember."

"I'll pick you up at seven twenty-five," Shoebag said. "Where will you be?"

"I'll sleep in the lily plant on the hall table," she said. "I'll be right there, waiting for you."

Shoebag took the stairs by twos, grinning happily as he jumped into his warm couch bed.

He went to sleep with dirty feet and a smile.

Seven

It had snowed in the night, so Mr. Biddle loaned Shoebag a pair of Pretty Soft's boots. They were made of white rubber, with white fur around the tops, lined with pink flannel stamped with pictures of little snowwomen.

Shoebag carried his shoes in a paper grocery bag with his lunch, his new pencil box, and lined writing pad.

Inside the pencil box was Drainboard, who'd told him she was very exhausted. She had had no sleep because the Persian cat from the third floor had gotten loose and sat staring at the lily plant in the downstairs hall for six hours.

"You know how smart cats are," Drainboard had told Shoebag. "And they are relentless, as well. That cat knew I was under one of the leaves, and she was ready to wait me out forever. . . . I hope I can stay awake, Son."

"It's all right if you nap," said Shoebag. "Just as long as I know you're with me, that's what counts."

As they trudged through the snow, down Beacon Hill, Mr. Biddle gave Shoebag twenty-five cents to purchase milk for lunch. He told Shoebag he was going to buy him boots, and a little briefcase, earmuffs, gloves, and a warm wool scarf.

"Nothing but the best for you, Son!" he said jovially. "By this time tomorrow you'll have everything a young man needs."

"Thank you, Mr. Biddle."

"Call me Dad, okay? You are my new son."

"Okay, Dad."

Shoebag kept one hand in the pocket of his new red wool jacket. He had the hood pulled over his head.

"See that park over there?" said Mr. Biddle. "That's where Pretty Soft will go today with Madam Grande de la Grande, when the Zap man comes. It is the only time she leaves the house, except when she goes to the television studio to make a new commercial."

"She only leaves the house once a month?"

"Yes, so you must remember everything that happens today at school, and tell her all about it. I know nothing bad will happen, so I do not have to remind you of the rule."

"Oh, I know the rule," said Shoebag. "Never discuss bad things."

44

"Never!" Mr. Biddle agreed, and his mustache wiggled as he smiled down at Shoebag.

The principal of The Beacon Hill Elementary School was a small, round, fat fellow with a face the color of a tomato, and no hair on his head.

"I am pleased to meet you, Stuart Bagg," he said.

"My name is Mr. Doormatee. Always remember that the word principal ends in *p a l,* and that's what I am, too, your pal."

Then, as Mr. Biddle left to go to the department store he managed, Shoebag was told to go into the cloakroom and take off his boots and his coat.

On his way there, Shoebag got the pencil box out of the paper bag. "Okay, Mama?"

"Shoebag, if your father ever hears that you are calling a person "Dad," it will be the end of his patience with you."

"What am I to do?" Shoebag asked. "He is buying me boots, a little briefcase, earmuffs, gloves, and a warm wool scarf."

"He is trying to buy a son," said Drainboard. "You cannot buy a son . . . and don't you ever call that lady with the gigantic appetite, who paints the sea, mother."

"What shall I give them as a reason I cannot call them those names?" Shoebag asked his mother.

"Say you have a family, that's all," she said, and then she fell asleep between a red and a yellow pencil, for she was still exhausted.

Shoebag sat down in a little chair and started taking off his boots.

"Tee hee!" a boy's voice said. "Look what the new kid is wearing! Girl's boots!"

"Only until tomorrow," said Shoebag. "Tomorrow I will have my own boots."

"Tomorrow is not today, though," the boy said. "What is your name, little girl?"

"I am a little boy and my name is Stuart Bagg."

"Stuart is not a proper name for a little girl," said the boy. "We'll call you Stuella."

Then the boy called out to the others, "Come and meet the new little girl, Stuella Bagg. Isn't she pretty? She has white fur boots with little snow-women inside!"

"You are a mean little boy," said Shoebag.

"I am a mean big boy," the boy replied, and he was right, for when he got up from the little chair he was not only tall, but also husky. He had long hair as black as midnight, and large white teeth. Very dark brown eyes squeezed together like slits, and he had a squashed-in nose from fighting.

"My name is Tuffy Buck," he said, "and I am boss of this cloakroom! I am also boss of the recess yard, and boss of all the slides and swings in the recess yard! I am boss of all the blocks that surround this school, and boss of the cafeteria!"

Shoebag did not know what to say to that, so he said nothing.

"Say hello to Stuella Bagg!" Tuffy Buck shouted, and one by one, boys and girls began calling out, "Hello, Stuella . . . Hello, Stuella . . . Hello, Stuella."

"Say hello back," Tuffy Buck commanded Shoebag.

"Hello," said Shoebag, and he felt something very strange happening in his eyes. They began to hurt and they began to fill with liquid. That morning when he had awakened with moisture on his forehead and under his arms, Mrs. Biddle had said he was sweating from too many blankets.

"Crybaby!" said Tuffy Buck. "Now I know you're a little girl, because you're crying."

"I'm not crying," Shoebag said. "My eyes are sweating a little, that's all."

"Stuella with the sweating eyes!" said Tuffy Buck, and everyone laughed and laughed.

After that, no one wanted to make friends with Shoebag. No one wanted to get on the bad side of Tuffy Buck.

When the bell for lunch rang, Shoebag stayed at his desk while everyone filed out of the room.

"Mama?" he whispered into his pencil box. "What am I going to do? Nobody in this school likes me."

When there was no answer, Shoebag opened his pencil box a crack, and saw that Drainboard was still sound asleep between the red and yellow pencils.

He did not have the heart to wake her up, and

in a way he was glad she had slept through everything, for she would only have felt like a helpless cockroach who had always known people were cruel.

Shoebag put the pencil box inside the grocery bag with his lunch, and trudged down to the cafeteria. He had no appetite, and he had no wish to go into that big bright room with all the tables and chairs, and everyone finding friends to eat with. But what could he do?

He stood in line to buy chocolate milk. He noticed that certain boys and girls pushed ahead of him, laughing, telling others, "Stuella doesn't care if we go before her! Come on!"

By the time he finally got his chocolate milk, nearly everyone had plates of food in front of them, or their sandwiches out of their baggies and bitten into. No one called him over to a table the way others had been invited to join groups. He finally found a table that was half full, at which sat others like him: the ones who weren't liked. There was the boy they called Fatso, with his face in a sardine sandwich. There was the girl known as The Ghost, who was skeletal thin with skin the color of flour. Bark was there, the small boy who was terrified of all dogs. And so was Handles there, the boy with ears which stuck way out. The girl called Two Times sat there, so nervous she said everything twice.

Shoebag sat down with them. No one said anything to him, and he did not try to start a conversation.

When was it? Toward the end of lunch when the scream came out of The Ghost? What a scream it was! "YEEEEEEEEEEEEE-OWWWWWWW! A ROACH!"

Shoebag heard the scream before he caught a glimpse of his mother crawling near the bottom of the bag containing his salami sandwich.

Salami had always been irresistible to Drainboard. She never got a taste of it, either, when Under The Toaster was around, for it was his most favorite choice morsel.

The scent of it must have awakened her, and while Shoebag had not yet taken his sandwich out of the bag, she must have been sneaking in there for a taste.

"YEEEEEEEEEEOWWWWWWW! A COCK-ROACH!" The Ghost cried again.

Everyone at Shoebag's table jumped out of their chairs, and soon the whole cafeteria was in an uproar.

And there, of course, in the center of all the action, stood Tuffy Buck.

"So Stuella, you have brought cockroaches from home!"

By this time, Drainboard had disappeared.

"There was only one!" Fatso said.

"*Only one?*" Tuffy Buck exclaimed. "That's one too many to suit the boss of the cafeteria! Where is it? Would you like to eat it, Fatso?"

"Make *him* eat it," Fatso pointed to Shoebag. "He brought it to school. I didn't."

"Where is it?" Tuffy Buck said.

Then a voice Shoebag had never heard before said, "I stepped on it. It's gone." At the same time this boy said those words, and just as Shoebag began to feel his eyes hurt again, and the moisture come, he looked down and saw a hand nudging him, with two fingers crossed. Shoebag happened to know that signal, from watching people over the years. That signal meant: I am fibbing.

Tuffy Buck could not see the signal.

He said, "Good for you, Gregor! We can always count on you to show up out of nowhere and save the day!"

Shoebag looked up at this boy Gregor, and he knew then why Tuffy Buck's voice was suddenly so polite.

Gregor was taller than Tuffy, and he was huskier, too. He was also mysterious, for he wore very dark glasses, the kind with mirror lenses in which you saw your own reflection. And he had a strange long nose, with a twitch to it, as though he was catching the scent of something wild. His hair was so short it was almost like a beard on his head, a bristle, and it was blacker even than Tuffy's, blacker than midnight. But the spookiest thing about him was his voice, which was not as loud as it was deep, like a grown man's.

"All right, the roach is gone!" said this peculiar fellow. "Everybody move away!"

"You heard what Gregor said," Tuffy told the other boys and girls. "Everybody move away!"

And everybody did. They all went back to their tables and their food, except for The Ghost, who had long ago run from the cafeteria in hysterics.

Gregor sat down in her chair. He put a Sony Watchman down on the table, and turned it on to the noon news. Then he stuck out a large, long-fingered hand. "I am Gregor Samsa," he said.

"I am Stuart Bagg." Then Shoebag had to whisper and find out, "You didn't really step on the roach?"

"I don't step on things," Gregor Samsa answered.

"Where did you come from?" Shoebag asked him.

"I come from here and there. I go back and forth. I smelled your sandwich."

"Would you like half?" Shoebag asked him.

"Would I!"

Bark spoke up then. "Even though a roach was near it?"

"Roaches have been around for 250 million years," Gregor Samsa answered. "They were here 249 million years before people were." He reached over and took the sandwich.

"I know that, but how did you know that?" said Shoebag. "Not many people know that."

51

Fatso joined the conversation. "He knows that because he watches television all the time, and he never forgets a fact."

"He memorizes everything," said Bark.

"He learned the part in the new school play just like that," said Handles, snapping his fingers.

"He doesn't have to come to regular rehearsals," said Fatso. "Only dress rehearsal."

Gregor Samsa took an enormous bite from the sandwich half, and changed the TV channel to a movie.

"Do you ever stop watching television?" Shoebag asked him.

"Om uddyin me man mactor."

"What?" Shoebag asked.

Bark answered for Gregor. "He says he's studying to be an actor, Stu."

So for the first time, he heard a classmate call him by a boy's name, and all because of Gregor Samsa.

"I bet Tuffy would have made me eat the dirty cockroach if it wasn't for you, Gregor," said Fatso.

Gregor was busy eating, and watching TV, his nose twitching, his forehead furrowed.

"Too bad you're not around more, Gregor," Fatso said.

Shoebag could not resist peeking into Gregor's mirrored eyeglasses. What Shoebag saw in the lenses was his true self: the antennae, the six legs, the shiny brown shell.

"Why isn't Gregor around more?" he asked Fatso.

Gregor himself answered. "When I'm here, I wish I was there, and when I'm there, I wish I was here. I keep going back and forth.

"He keeps skipping school," Two Times spoke up. "He keeps skipping school."

Then the bell rang and lunch was over.

Shoebag threw his paper bag in the trash can on the way out of the cafeteria. He checked the inside of his pencil box.

There was Drainboard, straddling the metal compass.

She said, "I'm sorry, Son, if I caused a commotion. Hard Italian salami is my downfall."

"I think I made a friend, Mama," Shoebag said.

"Remember, though, honey, people will turn on you. You can't ever trust them."

"But one just saved your life, Mama!"

"That was very unusual, Shoebag. I guess there's an exception to every rule."

"Go back to sleep, Mama. Good night, sleep tight, don't let the bedbugs bite."

"What bedbugs?" Drainboard hopped up on all sixes with her antennae quivering.

Shoebag grinned. "It's just an expression," he said.

At the end of the school day, when Shoebag went down to the cloakroom, took off his shoes, and stuck his feet into the white fur boots, he felt something in the left one.

It was a piece of folded paper, which he took out, opened, and read.

When Gregor is here, you have nothing to fear,
But everyone knows that he comes and goes,
So wait for the day when Gregor's away,
Then I'll be nearby and Stuella will cry!

Eight

That first Monday of every month, when the Zap man came, Pretty Soft and Madam Grande de la Grande stayed in the park until The Beacon Hill Elementary School let out. Pretty Soft never swung on the swings or went down the slides, for she could not chance falling and getting a bruise or a black and blue mark.

Just as the children came running toward the swings and the slides, Madam Grande de la Grande always said, "Oh, dear, dear, dear. Here they come. Here come the civilians! And you know what *they* might do."

"They might tell me bad things," Pretty Soft would say, "or they might recognize me and feel jealous because they are not television stars. We had better hurry home!"

"They might ask you for your autograph, too," Madam G. de la G. would say. "My, how they pestered me for mine when I was Glorious Gloria de la Grande! I could not eat out anywhere, or walk my little bulldog, or shop, or sit in the sun, but one of them showed up, autograph book in hand, pen thrust into my face! Oh, dear, oh, dear, it was dreadful how they loved me!"

That day, before any little civilians showed their faces, Madam was tutoring Pretty Soft in charm.

"Never say what you think," she said, "and never mean what you say. . . . And remember to give a compliment of some sort, one a conversation."

"What kind of compliment?" Pretty Soft asked.

"Nothing serious, child. Say, 'You have such good taste in clothes,' or say, 'You have the most interesting eyes.' Say, 'My, you're amusing!' or say, 'This conversation has given me so much to think about.' "

"Could I say, 'I like your eyeglasses'?" Pretty Soft asked.

"If they are unusual, yes. But phrase it with more flair, dear. Say, 'I simply cannot take my eyes off your eyeglasses! They are simply splendid!' "

After that suggestion, Pretty Soft's mind wandered during the rest of the charm lesson. She was imagining herself complimenting a certain big boy with dark glasses and a long nose, who sometimes appeared in the park with the Beacon Hill Elementary School civilians.

She did not know his name, or anything about him. She and Madam Grande de la Grande would be leaving the park just as he arrived. He never seemed to notice Pretty Soft, perhaps because she looked so young. She would hear him calling out in this very, very deep voice, "Let the little kids have the swings!" or "It's Fatso's turn on the slide!"

He always carried a Sony Watchman in one hand, but what drew Pretty Soft to him was his eyeglasses, which were like mirrors.

Whenever Pretty Soft passed him, she'd whisper to the lenses, "I see my own beauty, may it last forever."

So in her daydreams of him, there on the park bench that freezing cold afternoon in March, Pretty Soft gave him the compliment, and he said . . . and he said . . . And Pretty Soft was stuck.

"Madam," she said, just as three little girls her own age came skipping into the park, "how do young civilians talk?"

"Come, child, it's time to go home," said Madam, gathering her black cape around her and tossing one end of her bright red scarf over her shoulder. "Don't worry about how any civilians talk. They seldom say anything worth remembering. . . . Oh, to me, to *me*, of course, they were obsequious. That means they groveled and blushed, and they said things like 'Gloria Glorious, you are a wonderful person,' which is worth remembering, perhaps, but not well put. Not imaginative. . . . Come, child.

57

We'll finish your lesson in charm another time."

"I know how I can find out about young civilians," said Pretty Soft. "I have Stuart Bagg to talk to now."

And sure enough, when they returned to the apartment house, which smelled of Fresh Meadow Scent to disguise the Zap fumes, there was Stuart Bagg.

"Achoo!" sneezed Madam Grande de la Grande, who was allergic to Fresh Meadow Scent. "I would rather smell Zap than this sickly sweet odor your mother sprays everywhere!"

"It smells like too many flowers," said Stuart Bagg, who was trying on new clothes Mr. Biddle had left for him.

"There can never be too many flowers," Madam Grande de la Grande said into the handkerchief she held to her nose. "On my opening nights you could not find a place to stand in my dressing room, for all the floral tributes. The florists had to send to other cities for them, there were so many orders."

Pretty Soft watched Stuart Bagg prance around the dining room trying things on, and swinging his new schoolbag. She listened to him tell about buying chocolate milk for lunch and eating with five other children in the school cafeteria.

"Achoo! Achoo!" Madam Grande de la Grande sneezed, then asked him if he'd learned arithmetic, or practiced writing, or read a poem?

"There *was* a poem," he said.

"What was it about?" Madam asked him.

Stuart Bagg looked at Pretty Soft, then back at Madam.

He said, "Oh, it was just this happy poem about seeing someone again someday."

Pretty Soft said, "I like to eat alone, or with Madam. And I don't like poems about seeing people again, so I wouldn't have enjoyed myself at Beacon Hill Elementary School."

Now that they were upstairs in Pretty Soft's pink bedroom, and Stuart Bagg was still downstairs, Madam Grande de la Grande spoke up.

"You could have told Stuart Bagg his new brown boots were too divine for words, or that he looked dashing in his new brown earmuffs, new pigskin gloves, and new warm blue wool scarf. . . . Achoo! That would have been practicing charm. Also, a charming person never says she does not like things that her conversational partner has expressed an interest in — Achoo!"

Madam was still in her black cape and fire red scarf, for she would be going home any minute.

"He knows he looks good in his new clothes," said Pretty Soft. "Look at the way he danced around the dining room table!"

"But people, civilians in particular, like to hear they look good," said Madam. "Heaven knows they don't ever get any applause, camera close-ups, or critics' raves."

"Then *you* should have complimented him," said Pretty Soft.

"Dear Girl, I am already charming. And *I* do not have to worry about shooting another Pretty Soft commercial next month. . . . Just remember that clever little Claudia Clapper is waiting in the wings for the day she can take your place."

"But I have Mildred, and she doesn't have a cat," said Pretty Soft.

"Cats and actors are replaced as easily as light bulbs, child, and don't forget it. You need to practice being charming. Achoo! You're out-of-touch with charm!"

She pulled the cape's hood up over her orange-red hair, and said, "*Adieu!* Farewell! Until we meet again — *Adiós!*"

Pretty Soft settled down on her bed and reached for the television remote. She kept the sound down low, for she was not interested yet in what was on the screen. She did her eye exercises, her arm exercises, and the ones for keeping her chin muscles strong.

Then she stared into space and thought of the big boy with the dark glasses and the long nose.

What if she had said to him, "I simply cannot take my eyes off your eyeglasses! They are splendid!"

He might have walked right by her again, without

answering, which could have hurt her feelings, and certainly would have caused her to frown.

Pretty Soft jumped off her bed and went out into the hall. She crept up to the third floor, where another family lived. There was something up there which was as pretty and soft as she was. Often, late at night, when everyone was asleep, she went to get it. Now she felt like having it, because of all that Madam had said. She would rather not think about it. She needed something to take her mind off the April shoot of the Pretty Soft commercial, too.

Pretty Soft opened the door to the apartment on the third floor and called, "Mildred! Mildred!"

Of course, the Persian cat did not come running. Why run when you could sit right behind the door, and let someone call your name and call your name and wonder where you were?

"Mildred? MIL-dred!"

After a while the Persian cat peeked around the corner, but of course she did not look Pretty Soft in the eye. She looked beyond Pretty Soft as though whatever she was interested in seeing was off in the distance, not down on all fours begging her to come out.

"There you are, Mildred!" Pretty Soft clapped her hands and smiled, reaching out for the soft, brown and gold fur.

Pffft! The cat ran past her, down the stairs, full

speed ahead, darting into the first open door, which led into Pretty Soft's bedroom.

Under the bed she went, waiting for Pretty Soft to try and find which piece of furniture she'd escaped under.

Pretty Soft returned and shut the door.

"Why were you downstairs in the hall all last night, Mildred?" Pretty Soft asked. "If you'd come up and scratched on my door, I would have put you back in your house."

Pretty Soft got up on her bed.

"I know you're in here somewhere, Mildred, and you'll have to show yourself if you want to go home."

Nothing.

Pretty Soft said, "Certain Persian cats are dying to be petted but they won't admit it, so they sit in the dust balls, under things, and where does that get them?"

Nothing.

"You had better practice being charming, Mildred. . . . Just you remember that a slinky Siamese cat is waiting in the wings to take your place next month."

That would not work on Mildred. Pretty Soft realized it as soon as the words were out of her mouth. Mildred did not relish being a spokescat on national television. It meant being carried to the studio in her cat case, having butter-coated dope pills thrust down her throat, and drooping through the day under bright lights, too weak and powerless to hiss at or scratch the people who picked her up.

Now across the room, on the television screen, came the chorus of toilet paper rolls dancing merrily down the green hill, unfurling amid buttercups and brown-eyed Susans as they sang.

Pretty Soft turned up the sound on the TV remote. "Here we are, Mildred!"

Six hundred sheets a roll, and soft as any kitty,
We're double-layered, too, and people say we're pretty.
We come in shades of blue and beige, green, yellow, and . . .

Mildred settled down to snooze and dream of the cockroach she had known was in the downstairs hall the night before, under the lily leaves.

Nine

Pretty Soft? May I come in?" Shoebag asked.
"Please do," said Pretty Soft, "but you just missed my commercial."

The moment Shoebag stepped inside, the Persian cat from the third floor came out from under her bed.

"That cat has escaped from upstairs!" Shoebag said.

"Mildred doesn't escape," said Pretty Soft. "I let her out. Don't pay attention to her or she'll hide again."

The cat went directly to Shoebag, and as he walked around the room, she walked a few feet behind him.

"Stop following me around!" said Shoebag. "I don't like cats!"

"Mildred doesn't really like people, either," Pretty Soft said, "and I've never seen her follow someone around that way."

"Tell her to stop!" Shoebag said.

"She won't do anything anyone tells her to, unless you dope her. Then she just acts dumb and sleepy."

"Dope her then!" said Shoebag, while the cat continued following him.

"I can't dope her. I don't have her pills. The television people are the only ones who dope her, so they can film our commercial."

"Maybe if I sit down she'll go away," said Shoebag. He sat in the pink chair across from the bed.

Mildred sat beside the chair, staring up at him.

"She never does that," said Pretty Soft. "Maybe you have a bug on you. That's the way she acts if there's a bug around or a mouse."

Shoebag had let Drainboard out of the pencil box an hour ago. She had gone to help the family move back from the house next door, where they'd waited while the Zap man was in this one.

"I don't think there are any live bugs left," said Pretty Soft. "Maybe there's a mouse somewhere."

Mildred would not take her eyes off Shoebag.

"Put her back upstairs where she belongs," he said.

"I like her," Pretty Soft said. "I never get to really look at her because she's always hiding."

"Shoo! Beat it!" Shoebag waved his hands at her and stamped his feet.

The cat did not budge.

"Just ignore her," Pretty Soft said. "Just talk to me and don't pay any attention to her."

"But she makes me nervous!" Shoebag said.

Pretty Soft picked up her pink mirror and handed it to Shoebag.

"You're no fun when you're nervous. Look in the mirror and say what I say, and you won't be nervous," Pretty Soft said.

"I can't say I see my own beauty. I'm not a beautiful person."

Mildred watched him.

Pretty Soft said, "Then say 'I see my own cuteness,' because you *are* cute, Shoebag."

Shoebag liked it that she called him by his real name. She always called him Stuart Bagg around other people. He also liked hearing that he was cute, something no one had ever said to him before.

"I'll try anything to keep from being nervous," he said.

He picked up the mirror and told it, "I see my own cuteness, may it last forever."

The cockroach reflection trembled.

And why not? With that terrible Persian cat sitting there licking its chops.

Pretty Soft could see that her mirror trick did not work for Shoebag. He was still wringing his hands and now his forehead was breaking out in sweat.

"We have to relax you or you're no fun to be with," she said. "We can read my diary. *You* can read it aloud."

"But your father said no one ever reads other people's diaries or journals, that they're private."

"You are my new little brother, aren't you?" Pretty Soft smiled. She took out a small pink book from under her pillow. She passed it to Shoebag, who had to reach over Mildred's head to get it. "Start at the beginning. January 1," said Pretty Soft.

Shoebag opened "My Diary" and began to read.

January 1
Dear Diary,
    Cold today. Madam Grande de la Grande not here. Pretty Soft commercial played three times in afternoon, so I earned $450.

January 2
Dear Diary,
    Cold today. Madam Grande de la Grande here. Pretty Soft commerical played two times in afternoon, so I earned $300.

January 3
Dear Diary,
    Snow and cold today. Madam Grande de la Grande here. Pretty Soft commercial played three times in afternoon, so I earned $450.

Shoebag looked across at Pretty Soft and said, "But you write the same thing over and over, and it's only about the weather, Madam Grande de la Grande, and how much you made."

"Skip to the first Monday of the month," she said. Shoebag found it.

January 5
Dear Diary,
Snow and sleet. Madam Grande de la Grande and I go to park. Missed all but one Pretty Soft commercial, but think I earned at least $150.

Shoebag sighed.

"What's the matter?" Pretty Soft asked him.

"Don't you ever write about anything else?"

"You just read that I went to the park on the fifth of January. What do you want?"

"Don't you ever write about your feelings?"

"If it's cold, I feel cold, don't I? If I'm making money, I feel rich, don't I?"

"I guess so," said Shoebag. "I suppose so," he said.

"This conversation has given me so much to think about," said Pretty Soft.

"What has it given you to think about?" Shoebag asked.

"I was just being charming."

"Maybe that's why I'm not nervous anymore," Shoebag told her.

Because for a while, anyway, Shoebag had forgotten that the cat was still there, and still watching Shoebag's every move.

Ten

Time always does one thing: Time passes. It passes for people, and for cockroaches, for jumping spiders, and for Persian cats.

Time passing always does one thing: It changes people, and it changes cockroaches. It changes jumping spiders, and it even changes Persian cats.

In time, Mr. and Mrs. Biddle began to count Shoebag as a permanent member of the family. Mrs. Biddle washed and ironed his clothes, and packed a lunch for him every school day. Mr. Biddle gave up his office alcove and turned it into a bedroom for Shoebag.

At school, Tuffy Buck got meaner and meaner, and in addition to being boss of the cloakroom, the recess yard, the cafeteria, boss of all the slides and swings in the recess yard, and all the blocks that surround the school, he also became boss of the Beacon Hill Park.

Gregor Samsa had not been seen again, so every

day Shoebag went to school he was picked on, called Stuella, and left poems telling him the next day would be even worse.

Of course, he could not say anything about this to Pretty Soft, because of the rule. When he mentioned it to Mr. Biddle, Mr. Biddle had this answer. "At that school, they do not think you belong to anyone. If you would let me call you Son, and if you would call me Dad, things might be different."

But Shoebag could not do that, for he had promised his mother he would stop it, and he had.

He had told the Biddles that someday, when his memory came back, he would find his real parents, and they would not like him calling other people Mom and Dad or letting them call him Son.

Shoebag turned out to be a good student and Mr. Doormatee kept telling him so, and reminding him that his name ended in pal.

"But I am picked on, sometimes," Shoebag told him, "and I have no pal then. I am called by a girl's name, and I have no pal then."

"Girls are as good as boys," said Mr. Doormatee, "so you should not object to being called by a girl's name, Stuart Bagg."

"But I am a boy."

"Then learn to stand up for yourself. Learn to box, or wrestle. Tell the coach to teach you. Tell him I'm your pal."

What the coach told Shoebag was, "You *need* a

pal, Stuart Bagg. You punch like a kitten and you wrestle like a fish."

Madam Grande de la Grande grew more and more anxious about Pretty Soft's next shoot, and if she would have charm.

Once, she took Shoebag aside.

"Do you realize that if she loses her spokesgirl job, you'll be just another mouth to feed in this house, young man?"

"What can *I* do to help her?" Shoebag asked.

"Act like a winner. Tell her how popular you are at school, and how you are better than anyone in everything. Then, always lose any game you play together. If she wins a game from a winner, she will feel like the biggest winner of all."

"She is already practicing her charm," Shoebag said.

"And so she should," said Madam Grande de la Grande. "She must be charming, confident, and beautiful to beat out Claudia Clapper . . . and Claudia Clapper is younger, too. The young ones come along and snatch the dream right out of your heart, Stuart Bagg. I've seen it happen!"

There were other changes, too.

Shoebag had two cousins move in a box from Atlanta, Georgia, and the very day they arrived, the jumping spider ate them. The spider was changing very fast himself. He was almost as fat as his hairy brown brother from next door.

When the Persian cat got loose, her only interest was stalking Shoebag. Now she would not only sit and stare at him, but she would reach out and cuff his leg with her paw, or jump up on the arm of his chair and move her jaws at him and drool.

Under The Toaster had changed so much he hardly spoke to Shoebag. He had other sons now, Shoebag's new little brothers, who ran from him, and did not believe he was their brother. There was Coffee Cup, Wheaties Box, and Radio.

"They look exactly like me!" Under The Toaster said often, and proudly. "They're clean and they're quiet, too!"

Drainboard had been terrified by a narrow escape from the jumping spider's dragline. He had twisted it twice around her cerci and told her, "Your new name is Supper, for that's what you will be in a few hours. My supper." It had been a miracle that she was able to wiggle loose and run to safety up under the long white strings of the mop.

Still, nights the jumping spider would croon out in the darkness, "I feel like having 'Supper' soon."

Drainboard could not understand why Shoebag would not kill him and protect their home sweet home.

"All the years we wished that he was dead," she told Shoebag, "and now you can kill him, but you won't!"

"I'm not that much of a person yet," Shoebag kept insisting, but he felt like a coward and a traitor.

*   *   *

Of all the changes in the passing of time, Pretty Soft had changed the most. When Shoebag would tell her how popular he was at school, and how he was better than anyone at everything, Pretty Soft would yawn and fidget. When Shoebag let her win at Monopoly and all the Nintendo games hooked into her television, Pretty Soft would complain.

"It's no fun to play with someone so dumb!"

"I'm not dumb, you're just smarter, Pretty Soft. You're a winner," Shoebag said. "You are such a big winner that you are able to beat the most popular boy in Beacon Hill Elementary school, the one who is better than anyone at everything!"

Pretty Soft shot him a look of disgust. "That is civilian talk, Shoebag. It is obsequious, which means groveling and fawning."

"I'm sorry," said Shoebag, who could not seem to please her anymore, or stop her worrying about shooting her new commercial.

"My, you're amusing!" said Pretty Soft.

"But you just said — "

She did not let him finish. "I have to give one compliment a conversation," she told him. "I have to be charming or Claudia Clapper will get my job!"

73

Eleven

One fine day in April, Mr. Doormatee stood up in assembly and read a page Tuffy Buck had written about his father. Mr. Buck had gone on a hunt for alligators down in Florida, and he had killed four of them himself.

Everyone in school clapped their hands, and Mr. Doormatee said, "Congratulations to your father, Tuffy. Children? When you pass Tuffy in the hall today, say to him, 'Congratulations to your father!' "

Before assembly was over, Mr. Doormatee reminded everyone that principal ended in pal, and that on their way out, they should drop some pennies in the Save The Seals can, "because we all know that a seal needs a pal, too."

Shoebag was happy to give the three pennies he had left from his milk money to the seals. Still, something bothered him, and he mentioned it to Fatso as they walked down to the cloakroom.

"If people save seals, why do they kill alligators?"

"Seals are like panda bears and koalas — they're cute. Alligators are like snakes and rats — they're ugly."

Shoebag thought of Pretty Soft saying he was cute.

Fatso continued, "If you're ugly, people turn against you."

"But how do people decide what's ugly?" Shoebag asked.

"People don't decide, they just see you and they know. If you're an animal, it's better to be soft and furry. It isn't good to slither around without legs, or to live behind things and have a long tail."

"What about bugs?" Shoebag asked. "What about bugs with legs and antennae."

"Legs, maybe, if the bugs have nice colors, like ladybugs with red on them, and green walking sticks. But antennae, *never!* Bugs with antennae get stepped on! So do bugs who live behind or under things!"

"But why?" said Shoebag.

Fatso shrugged sadly and said, "Don't ask me of all people. If Mr. Buck was out on a people hunt, and he saw us walking down this hall together, I'd be the one he'd go after."

"Because I'm cute?" Shoebag asked.

"Because you're thin, and I'm fat."

"It doesn't seem fair to judge everything by looks," Shoebag said.

"Who's talking about what's fair?" Fatso said, and then at the approach of Tuffy Buck, he called out "Congratulations to your father!"

Tuffy was surrounded by kids saying the same thing, and it was hard to know if he had heard Fatso.

"I'm not taking any chances," Fatso told Shoebag. "I want to stay on the good side of him."

"I didn't think he had a good side," Shoebag said, "and I'm not sending congratulations to Mr. Buck. I'm for the poor alligators."

"That won't get you anywhere," Fatso said.

Shoebag said, "I'm for the alligators and the snakes and the rats, and the bugs with legs and antenna, and everything that lives behind and under things!" Then he thought of the jumping spider and he added, "Unless one makes himself my enemy!"

"What about the seals and the pandas, the koala bears, and the bugs with color?"

"I'm for them, too, and for you, Fatso. I'm for you, too."

"Thanks, Stuart Bagg," said Fatso, "but I'm not even for me."

"How can you not be for yourself?" Shoebag asked him.

"It's very risky to be for yourself," Fatso told him. "If you are, you have to stick up for yourself. That's too hard."

When they got to the cloakroom, while they were getting into their coats, Tuffy Buck appeared again in a group of kids who were patting him on the back, and punching his arm with friendly jabs.

"Congratulations to your father!" Fatso called out again.

"I heard you the first time!" Tuffy snarled.

Shoebag thought of the alligators, the snakes, and the rats, and he thought of his very own family. He did not look across at Tuffy Buck, and he did not speak to him.

It was such a mild and sunny April afternooon that Shoebag did not feel like going directly home.

The other reason he did not feel like going directly home was that his father had told him not to come into the kitchen afternoons, since he only woke up Coffee Cup, Wheaties Box, and Radio.

"They need their sleep, they are just little tykes," Under The Toaster had said. "Have some consideration. Wipe your feet! You drag dirt around on floors we have to eat off! No wonder your little brothers can't believe you are one of us, the way you soil where we dine! They are afraid of you, besides."

"Tell them I'd never hurt my own brothers."

"I've told them that, but they just won't believe me."

"Maybe if you'd kill the jumping spider, they'd believe us," Drainboard had put in.

"Mama, you ask too much of me. I can not squash anything alive, not yet!"

"I'll be that spider's supper someday, Son."

77

Shoebag felt too guilty to face them all.

This was a good time to go to the park, too. Tuffy Buck was busy back at school receiving congratulations for his father.

Shoebag found an empty swing and got on it, closing his eyes as he made it go higher and higher. His legs were pointed at the sky, and he threw back his head and felt the sun warm on his face, as he sang to himself a favorite old cockroach song:

We lurk around and on our mark, we come
*   out in the dark,*
Hey de hi ho, we don't need a coach
To get there!
Hey de hi ho, if you are a roach,
You'll get there!

We creep around and find the crumbs, happy
*   to be chums,*
Hey de hi ho, we hunt high and low,
In kitchens,
Hey de hi ho, the parties we throw,
In kitchens!

Shoebag opened his eyes to enjoy his ride up toward the treetops, telling himself it was not so bad being a person, because the song had made him a little homesick.

What did he care that he was not snug as a bug napping with his new brothers in the warm dark, when there was a blue sky overhead, and off in the distance children playing in the sandboxes and . . . and . . . look, over there on that bench!

There they were! Madam Grande de la Grande and Pretty Soft!

He slowed himself down and began thinking of the date. Yes. The third. Monday . . . the first Monday in April.

He had forgotten that it was the very day the Zap man came.

"Hel-lo!" he called out to them. "Helllll-lo!"

Madam Grande de la Grande waved her red scarf at Shoebag and pointed him out to Pretty Soft.

Pretty Soft, naturally, did not let her mouth stretch in too wide a smile, for that would not be good for her face, but Shoebag could see all the way from the swings that she was watching him with interest.

He made himself go higher to show off, and then he let the swing lose momentum, twisting himself around as it slowed, winding himself in a half circle cleverly.

This was a glorious time, wasn't it? There were his friends over there, and here he was making the swing do graceful and funky things in the late afternoon sun.

"Hey de hi ho, we hunt high and low, In kitchens," he sang aloud.

He felt his feet scuff along in the dirt, worrying only a little that it might ruin his new shoes.

"Hey de hi ho, the parties we throw," he sang,

and then he did a fantastic little leap from the swing, knowing that Madam and Pretty Soft were watching him.

Next, a pair of hands grabbed his shoulders.

And next, a voice said, "Stuella! You didn't offer any congratulations to my father today, did you?"

Twelve

POW! WHUMP! WHUMP! WHUMP! POW!
"Oh, no!" said Pretty Soft. "Stuart Bagg is in a
fight! And he said he was popular with everyone!"

"There must be a policeman we can call to stop
this!" Madam Grande de la Grande cried out. She
got up from the park bench and looked up and
down Beacon Hill Park.

"Let's go closer," said Pretty Soft. "They are kick-
ing up so much dust rolling around over there on
the ground, I can't see anything!"

"Dust is not good for your nasal passages, child.
And it is not good for the eyes!"

"I've never seen a fight except on television."

"It could spill over on us, pet. I am going to look
for a policeman!" And with that, Madam trotted
away in her black cape, crying, "PO-LICE! PO-
LICE! Come quickly!"

Pretty Soft started over toward the swings, where

Shoebag was rolling around on the ground with a boy on top of him.

So this is a fight, live from Beacon Hill Park, Pretty Soft thought, and she was glad it had nothing to do with her.

Then as she was almost all the way to the slides, from out of nowhere, *he* appeared.

The tall one with dark glasses and a long nose.

"Break it up!" he was shouting as he ran in the direction of the fight.

Pretty Soft hurried after him. "Be careful. Dust is not good for the nasal passages, and it is not good for the eyes!"

Now the boy on top of Shoebag gave him a hard punch.

"This is for bringing a cockroach to school," and another, "and this is for not saying 'Congratulations to your father,' " and still another. "And this is what I'd give to Fatso, since he says you are sticking up for him now!"

The boy with the sunglasses stood over the pair. He put one hand on the boy holding Shoebag down in the dirt.

"Get off him, Tuffy Buck!" he said.

Tuffy Buck looked up, his eyes as wide as though he had seen something ghastly. "I'm s-s-sorry, Gregor."

Then he got off of Shoebag, and began slouching away, backward.

Gregor helped Shoebag to his feet.

"Are you all right, Bagg?"

"Yes," but Shoebag had a nosebleed.

Gregor got a wad of Kleenex from his pocket and passed it to Shoebag.

"Thanks," said Shoebag. "I am not a good fighter, and you are a pal. You are the only real pal I have!"

"That isn't what you told me," Pretty Soft stepped forward. "You lied to me, Stuart Bagg. You told me you were very popular, and better than anyone at everything!"

"I tried to keep you happy because of the rule," said Shoebag.

Gregor said, "What rule?"

"We have a rule that she can only hear and see things that are positive. We cannot let her become unhappy."

Pretty Soft said, "But I wouldn't have been unhappy if you'd told me you weren't popular, Stuart Bagg. Why would that have made me unhappy?"

Shoebag's face was suddenly scrunched up that awful way which made wrinkles and lines, and the Kleenex he held to his nose was bloody. "You aren't unhappy to know I'm not popular at school?" he asked Pretty Soft. "Are you unhappy to see the shape I'm in now?"

"I can't afford to be unhappy," she said.

"I know who you are," Gregor said. "You are

the little girl on television who sells toilet paper."

"I'm not as little as I look," said Pretty Soft. "I'm seven years old."

"You're Pretty Soft," he said. "I am Gregor Samsa."

While all of this was happening, Tuffy Buck was heading away from them on tiptoe, sneaking off unnoticed.

Gregor Samsa asked Pretty Soft, "Don't you feel badly that Stuart Bagg was just beat up?"

"I feel glad it's not happening to me," she said. "I have a new commercial to shoot very soon, and I must look my best and also be charming."

"But I'm your new brother," Shoebag said.

"I know you are," Pretty Soft said.

Gregor Samsa leaned down so his mirrored glasses were pointed right at Pretty Soft's sky-blue eyes. He spoke in his very, very deep voice. "I have thought of becoming a star myself, Pretty Soft, but now that I have met you, I know I could never be like you."

"You could practice," said Pretty Soft as she looked at the two mirrors that were his eyes.

"Even if I practiced I could never be so selfish. Even if I practiced I could never be so heartless," said Gregor Samsa. "No, I will have to be something else."

Then a most peculiar thing happened after he said that to Pretty Soft. She saw her reflection, but not her face: just its outline, not the eyes or nose, not the forehead or the mouth. It was an empty face.

Desperately, she said the words, "I see my own beauty, may it last forever."

"She says that when she's handling a crisis," Shoebag told Gregor Samsa.

"I don't see beauty," Gregor Samsa said. "I don't see anything."

"Don't say that to her!" Shoebag told him, and he went close to Pretty Soft, and put his arm around her.

"Please don't get blood on me, Shoebag." She said his real name, for she was rattled now. She put her hands to her face to feel her eyes and nose and mouth and forehead.

"I see my own beauty," she started to try again, but Gregor Samsa turned to face Shoebag.

"What did she just call you, Stuart Bagg?" he asked.

"I called him Shoebag. It's his nickname," said Pretty Soft. "Turn around and face me again."

Gregor ignored her. "That's not a nickname," he told Shoebag.

Pretty Soft knew then and there he did not know what he was talking about.

Down at the other end of the park, Madam appeared with a tall, uniformed policeman.

Pretty Soft hurried toward them, to announce that the fight was over, and to see her reflection in the mirror Madam always carried.

85

Yes! There she was again: everything in place on her beautiful face.

After the policeman had gone, and after Madam had put back the mirror in her bag, they strolled toward home.

"Is Shoebag a nickname or isn't it?" Pretty Soft asked.

"It is. A most unpleasant nickname," said Madam G. de la G.

"Am I selfish, Madam? Am I heartless?"

"Stars are the most unselfish of people," said Madam Grande de la Grande. "They give of themselves tirelessly. And no one has more heart than a star, child, for it is a star's responsibility to uncover the innermost secrets of the heart, and put them on display for all to see and applaud. . . . Oh, how I miss the applause! The shouts of Brava! Even the shrill whistles from the balcony!"

Pretty Soft decided not to ask the next question on her mind: how a nose, mouth, ears, and forehead could momentarily disappear from a face.

She must have imagined that.

Thirteen

I know a roach name when I hear one," said Gregor Samsa. He slung one arm around Shoebag's shoulder as they walked through the park.

"How come?" Shoebag asked.

"Oh, I go back and forth. I must have told you that. I go here and there . . . and when I am back, and when I am there, my own name is not Gregor Samsa. I am called In Bed. . . . Do you know what I am telling you?"

He gave Shoebag a long look, so long that Shoebag saw in the mirrored glasses the tiny black hairs on all six of his own legs, and his cerci.

"That means we were both born in warm, snug places," Shoebag said.

"And it is why we cannot step on things, too. We are neither of this world nor of that. But I plan to be in one place all the time, as soon as I decide which one."

He removed his arm from Shoebag's shoulder,

reached into his pocket and took out his Sony Watchman. "I watch the soaps in the afternoon," he said. "Do you mind?"

"Go right ahead."

"I cannot be without my TV, Shoebag. Do you know why?"

"Because you have your own little Watchman?"

"No, it's because I'm star struck. It's because I think there is no business like show business . . . or I did think that until a moment ago. Now I can see I may have to change my plans. Now I can see that even with practice I could not be that selfish or that heartless."

"But you are going to star in the school play, aren't you?"

"It may well be my last performance."

Shoebag felt sorry for his only real pal, because he sounded so downcast. Shoebag wanted to ask him more about when he was not Gregor Samsa, about when he was back and when he was there, and where exactly he was called In Bed. But first, Shoebag wanted to thank Gregor for saving him from Tuffy Buck again, and that was what Shoebag did.

Then Shoebag added, "You're lucky, too. You only have to look at him to make him stop being a bully. You never have to fight him."

"It's a good thing I don't. Our kind do not excel in fighting. We are a peaceable lot, satisfied with warm, dark places and our crumbs."

88

"You *are* lucky!" Shoebag said. "If Tuffy Buck knew you could not fight, he'd beat you up, too."

"It isn't luck I have. It's these glasses. People never see what their faces look like when they are being mean or petty. I come along when they are, and so they do. They can't believe they are seeing themselves. What they see stops them in their tracks.

"I should get glasses like that," said Shoebag.

"Only if you go back and forth and here and there," Gregor told him. "Dark glasses help your eyes adjust."

"When I go back, when I go there, I am still a little person," Shoebag told him.

"You must have dreamed very hard of being bigger."

"I did dream of being bigger."

"And something must have awakened you in the middle of that dream."

"The seven-legged, black jumping spider was letting down his dragline, right in the middle of my dream."

"Aha!" said Gregor. "You were not given the formula for going back. That comes at the end of the dream."

"And you? Were you given the formula?"

Gregor shook his head. "Do not ask me for it, though, even though I am your only real pal. If I tell it to you, it loses its power for me."

Gregor was playing with the Watchman, channel-hopping as they ambled through the park.

"I would give anything to see my old familiar self again," said Shoebag, "somewhere besides in mirrors."

"Maybe you will. You'll see. You'll see."

"What will I see, Gregor? The Persian cat staring at me with her jaws moving, *drooling?* Because she knows something, Mildred does. She is not fooled."

"You'll see. You'll see," said Gregor Samsa.

"What will I see? Tuffy Buck waiting for me tomorrow in the cloakroom? My own father complaining that I am too dirty to bear? Let me tell you, Gregor, let me tell you, In Bed, my life is not easy. There is the black jumping spider to worry about, too, and — " Shoebag stopped in midsentence, for suddenly he realized that he was walking through Beacon Hill Park talking to himself.

His only real pal had vanished.

Fourteen

Mrs. Biddle cooked a roast chicken for dinner that night, telling Shoebag that it was Pretty Soft's favorite meal.

While Shoebag set the table, he watched Mrs. Biddle taste the potatoes as she mashed them, and he thought of how Drainboard loved potatoes that way, particularly ones left in the pan and crusted over.

Stopping in the park had made him late getting home from school, so he had not seen his family that day.

"Tonight is a special occasion," said Mrs. Biddle, popping a spoonful of lima beans into her mouth. "We always celebrate the night before Pretty Soft goes to the television studio to make a new commercial. That makes her wake up happy, and when she is happy she looks her best."

"When will she have enough money saved so she doesn't have to work anymore?" Shoebag asked.

"She likes to work, Stuart, and college is very

expensive. Every year it costs more money to go to college. My parents never had enough money to send me."

"I guess I won't go, either," said Shoebag.

"Oh, there are always ways to get there if you're determined to go. Pretty Soft's just lucky she won't have to worry about all that."

"I will have to worry, I guess," said Shoebag.

"What you have to worry about right now is how to stay out of fights, and after dinner Mr. Biddle will help you."

When Pretty Soft came down to eat, she had adhesive tape near her mouth and near her eyes.

"How did *you* hurt *your* face?" Shoebag said, surprised.

Mr. Biddle said, "She didn't get hurt. She's just delighted about tomorrow, so she has to be careful not to smile too hard and leave lines."

"A big long white limousine is picking Mildred and me up tomorrow morning at seven-thirty, Stuart Bagg," said Pretty Soft as she helped herself to chicken with mashed potatoes and lima beans. "Madam Grande de la Grande will go to the studio with us and drill me in spelling, while I sit on the set waiting for them to shoot my commercial."

"She is wearing her new red-and-white polka dot dress," said Mrs. Biddle.

"They take an hour to put on her makeup," Mr. Biddle said.

"I have a director's chair with my name on it," said Pretty Soft, "and Mildred has a cat case with hers on it." She smiled across at Shoebag, then said, "Ouch! I've got to stop smiling this way. I just get so excited the night before a shoot!"

"She always has trouble getting to sleep on these nights, too," said Mrs. Biddle, "so you must be very quiet tonight, Stuart."

"I have lines to learn," Pretty Soft said. "I have to say to Mildred, 'Purrfection! That's Pretty Soft! The purrfect toilet tissue!' "

"You've already learned your lines then," said Mr. Biddle.

"But I say them over and over the night before," said Pretty Soft. "It is a star's responsibility to uncover the innermost secrets of the heart, and put them on display for all to see and applaud."

While Shoebag waited for the house to become quiet, so he could sneak down to visit his family, he wrote in his journal.

Mr. Biddle taught me some judo, to defend myself. "When anyone makes a grab for you," he said, "instead of ducking back, go forward to meet him." And he showed me a secret move to do. I am very homesick and wish I could go back and wish I could be there and wish I was me again.

The rain began just after the eleven o'clock news, when all the lights were off and everyone was in their bedrooms.

As Shoebag went downstairs, he could hear the distant thunder, and see the lightning through a window.

Drainboard always said nights like this were bad for late night picnics. People often got up to close windows, and to tell little children not to be afraid. Lights were turned on suddenly and bad storms made people too alert and active.

Was that why no one seemed to be around when Shoebag called out to them?

He felt his way in the dark, then stopped when he came to the kitchen stool.

He listened.

Since the Zap man had been there that day, Shoebag knew that all of roachdom was walking carefully to avoid cracks and crevices where the insecticide had been sprayed.

Very faintly he could hear a rustling and a murmur. Then what any roach most dreaded hearing, he heard: The Cockroach Prayer for The Dead.

"Go to a better life. Amen."

It was Under The Toaster's voice.

"Papa? Papa? It's me. Your son, Shoebag. Who died?"

"You dare to come to this memorial service?" said Under The Toaster. "You who would do nothing about the jumping spider? And now he has killed your little brother Coffee Cup."

"I hardly knew Coffee Cup. I only saw his two back legs once in my life, but I am terribly sorry, Papa."

"That's not all. Right this moment, rolled up in the dragline, way way up on the electric clock, is your mother! She is being saved for the jumping spider's breakfast!"

"I'll rescue her!" Shoebag cried out.

"Watch that hot breath of yours!" his father told him. "I am only a few feet away from you! How are you going to rescue her without a ladder?"

"I'll find a ladder!" Shoebag said, and an enormous roll of thunder shook the house.

Fifteen

Purrfection! That's Pretty Soft! the purrfect toilet tissue!"

Pretty Soft said her lines over and over to herself. Mildred was under the bed. She would probably never come out now that it was thundering. Pretty Soft had hoped to get some practice in, holding her at the right camera angle, but Mildred never cooperated, anyway, until the TV producer got the dope inside her. Then Mildred went limp, and you could do almost anything with her.

Pretty Soft did not mind the storm, but there was something she did mind late that night.

She could not forget what Gregor Samsa had said to her. Sometimes as she was practicing her part, the wrong words came to her head: words she should have spoken to him.

"If I was so selfish, would I be working my way through college?"

She should have said that.

Or she should have said, "If I didn't have a heart, how could I sell toilet paper to all of America?"

"Maybe *you* can't see anything in my face," she should have said, "but viewers can, or I wouldn't be a famous TV spokesgirl!"

Pretty Soft tried to put him out of her mind, but it was hard for her to put someone out of her mind who had mirrors for eyes. She decided to concentrate until all thoughts of him were gone.

"Purrrrfection!" she said again, aloud, "That's Pretty Soft! The purrrfect — "

Shoebag came running into her room without knocking.

"Go back outside and knock!" she told him.

"There isn't time! I need a ladder!"

"What is the matter with you, Shoebag? What if I'd been asleep, and you'd interrupted my beauty rest?"

"Pretty Soft, please! I need a ladder. The jumping spider has captured a roach and taken it up into the electric clock!"

"He probably wants it for his breakfast tomorrow," said Pretty Soft.

"But I must rescue it! I must capture it alive, to take to my science class tomorrow!"

"Madam Grande de la Grande would never let *me* study roaches," said Pretty Soft. "In *my* science lessons, I study caterpillars that turn into beautiful butterflies."

Now lightning danced across the sky through

97

Pretty Soft's window, and Mildred darted out from under the bed.

"There's no time for conversation!" said Shoebag. "What is Mildred doing loose?"

"I always keep her with me the night before we make a commercial. Otherwise, she hides in the morning, the moment I get her cat case out."

"Will you please, please help me find a ladder? What if the jumping spider gets hungry and eats the roach for a late night picnic?" Shoebag was wringing his hands and pacing up and down the room in his pajamas and robe.

Pretty Soft sat up straighter in her big pink bed.

"Is Gregor Samsa in your science class?"

"Of course he is!"

"Then I will get you the ladder if you promise one thing."

"Anything!" Shoebag was close to tears. Pretty Soft had never felt that intense about any of her science assignments.

"Promise me that you will tell Gregor Samsa I got the ladder for you."

"I promise you!" Shoebag said.

"Not many people would get out of bed in the middle of the night to do this," said Pretty Soft. "Only someone who is very unselfish would!"

"You are right, Pretty Soft! It is very unselfish of you!"

"Thank you, Shoebag," Pretty Soft said. "Fetch

me my robe over there on the chaise."

Down the stairs they went, with Mildred racing ahead of them.

"Why can't that cat stay back up in your room?" Shoebag said.

"Maybe she wants the jumping spider for her own late night picnic."

"If I told Gregor that you killed it for her, he would think that was unselfish, too," panted Shoebag, out-of-breath from running and from panic.

"He would know I was not heartless, too, if I would kill for Mildred."

"But how would you ever kill it?" Shoebag shouted over his shoulder as he hurried along.

"Easily! With a flyswatter!" said Pretty Soft. "There's one on a hook in the closet, right behind the ladder."

"Make sure you don't hurt the roach!"

"I'll go up on the ladder myself," said Pretty Soft. "I'll hand you down the roach, and then you pass the swatter up to me."

"You are a real pal, Pretty Soft!"

"Remember to tell Gregor that he is not your only pal, and that I am not selfish and heartless."

"Oh, I will, Pretty Soft, I definitely will!"

Shoebag helped Pretty Soft drag the ladder from the closet, across the floor, to the sink. The electric clock was directly above the sink.

"Go sit in the corner, Mildred!" Shoebag hollered

at the cat, who was nipping at his ankles.

"Shhh! You'll wake up Mom and Dad," Pretty Soft cautioned Shoebag, "and there is no sense telling Mildred to do anything. Cats do as they please!"

Mildred was sitting on the floor staring at Shoebag, her nose twitching.

"Hold the ladder firmly!" said Pretty Soft. "Once I did a commercial on a ladder. I was handing down rolls of toilet paper from a closet and I was saying — "

"Never mind all that now!" Shoebag said. "I am too nervous."

Pretty Soft went up the rungs slowly, singing her favorite song softly, under her breath, "Six hundred sheets a roll and soft as any kit-ty."

"Be careful of the roach!" Shoebag whispered loudly.

"I'm not even there yet! Look at all the dirty dishes mom left in the sink. You should wash them for her, Shoebag. I cannot do them for her, since it would give me dishpan hands."

Shoebag saw the crust of mashed potato on a pan, and said, "I'll leave them there tonight. I'll do them first thing in the morning."

After Shoebag got his mother safely inside his pocket, he would give her a treat.

The rain was heavy on the roof, and he hoped there would be no more thunder, nothing that could distract Pretty Soft from her rescue mission.

He hoped, too, that Under The Toaster was nearby watching. It would teach him that all people were not as cruel as he always said they were. And Drainboard — what would Drainboard think! Being saved from slaughter by a human being, for the second time!

Shoebag was smiling, and his heart was pounding.

"I see the roach all wrapped up," said Pretty Soft, "and I see the jumping spider!"

"Toss me the roach, please," Shoebag said, and in a moment his mother came sailing down, and he caught her in his hand.

"Blcch!" said Pretty Soft. "That was icky! My hands have sticky stuff on them!"

"That's just dragline silk," Shoebag reassured her. "Now let's get that spider!"

With Drainboard safely in his pocket he started to pass up the flyswatter.

But Mildred knocked it from his hand as she leaped up the ladder. She was after the jumping spider, who was racing up the wall.

Mildred's sudden move startled Pretty Soft and Shoebag.

Shoebag let go of the ladder for only a moment, but it was the very moment Pretty Soft tried to move out of Mildred's way.

The ladder swayed and fell to the kitchen floor, and Pretty Soft fell with it.

"Waaaaaaaaaaaaaa!" Pretty Soft was wailing.
"EEEEEEEE, OOOOOOOW!" went Mildred, who was clinging to the electric clock.

The jumping spider crawled behind a long fluorescent light bulb near the ceiling.

Sixteen

Next morning, Shoebag and Mr. Biddle were leaving for school when the long white limousine pulled up in front of the apartment building on Beacon Hill.

"I'm sorry," Mr. Biddle told the uniformed chauffeur, "but my daughter won't be going to the studio today. She is in no condition to be filmed."

Shoebag looked up at Pretty Soft's window, where Mildred sat in front of the pink curtains, licking a paw contentedly.

There was no sign of Pretty Soft.

She would not show herself, Shoebag knew. She had a worse black eye than Shoebag's, a swollen face, and puffed lip.

"Go now to Madam Grande de la Grande's," said Mr. Biddle, "and bring her back here. Pretty Soft needs her."

"There will be an extra charge for that," said the chauffeur. "That is not on my route."

"Just do it, please!" Mr. Biddle snapped, for all the Biddles, and Shoebag, too, had had no sleep, and were upset by Pretty Soft's terrible accident.

"I'll never work again!" Pretty Soft had cried. "They'll give the job to my stand-in, clever little Claudia Clapper!"

Only Mildred was pleased to see her carrying case put back inside Pretty Soft's closet. She had escaped being doped, and being subjected to the bright lights of the cameras. She was purring with joy, imagining the slinky Siamese cat taking over her role.

Shoebag was sad that Pretty Soft was in such bad shape, and that she had missed her appointment, but he could not help feeling delighted that he'd restored Drainboard to roachdom. And he had given her a generous helping of crusty mashed potatoes, too!

Never mind that the jumping spider was still loose! Shoebag had seen to it that his mother's life was saved!

As they walked down Beacon Hill together, Mr. Biddle said, "This was all your fault, Stuart, and I should be mad at you, but I'm not."

"I'm glad you're not. Why aren't you?"

"It's time for Pretty Soft to retire, that's why."

"I thought people didn't retire until they were sixty-five years old," said Shoebag, who had heard something like that over television once.

"Pretty Soft wouldn't have lived to be sixty-five

the way she was going. The whole thing got out of hand. Her mother and I thought it would be fun for her, and she could save her money for college, but soon it came to control her life. Enough is enough."

"Does that mean we don't have to follow the rule anymore?"

"It means the rule is out the window."

"What window is it out, sir?"

"That's just an expression, Stu. You have to bone up on your expressions. You're a little weak in that department."

As soon as Shoebag arrived in the cloakroom at school, he saw a note hanging from his coat hook.

What my father did to the alligator,
I'll do to you, a little later.

"Fatso? Have you seen Gregor this morning?" Shoebag asked in assembly.

"He's in the gym, where they're having a dress rehearsal of the school play," said Fatso. "Don't forget you're sticking up for me."

"I'll try," Shoebag told him.

"Don't just try, Stuart Bagg. Do it. You promised and I'm counting on you."

After Mr. Doormatee told everyone he was their pal, the children rose and recited a verse he led them in.

All things bright and beautiful,
All creatures great and small,
All things wise and wonderful,
The Lord God made them all.

"Remember that, boys and girls," said their principal, "and don't forget to drop your pennies in the can to save the seals."

Then Mr. Doormatee slammed his hand down on a fly that had been pestering him while he spoke.

"Got it!" he said.

As they sat having lunch in the cafeteria, Shoebag asked everyone in school who wasn't liked, "Here's a question for you. The good Lord made the bright and beautiful, the great and small, the wise and wonderful, but who made the rest of us?"

"The good Lord made the rest of us, too," said The Ghost, "but no one writes verses about it."

"That must mean all the writers are bright and beautiful, great and small, wise and wonderful," said Fatso, "or we'd be mentioned."

"We should write our own verses then," Shoebag said.

"How can ordinary people write?" said Bark.

"We wouldn't know how, know how," said Two Times.

"We aren't bright and we aren't beautiful," said Handles.

"Look at my face with the black eye and the

scratches, I look awful," said Shoebag, "but here's a line to rhyme:

"Looks aren't everything, this I know,"
Two Times laughed.
"Beauty won't last, it's like snow, it's like snow."
The Ghost said, "Who decides that I am dull?"
Fatso laughed. "Someone with a thicker skull."
"Ordinary people power!" Handles grinned.
Bark finished with, "This is now our shining hour!"

Never had the faces at that particular table in the school cafeteria glowed as they did at that moment.

"A toast!" said Shoebag raising his container of chocolate milk. "Here's to the rest of us. And here's to the rest of them!"

"Who's the rest of them?" Fatso asked.

"Alligators, snakes, rats, insects with antennae, things that live behind and under and in back of — our fellow critters that people step on, swat, and Zap!"

"I hope you don't mean things like mosquitoes?" said one at the table.

"I hope you don't mean flies, mean flies."

"And I hope you don't mean worms!"

"Well, I hope you don't mean bedbugs!"

"I just hope you don't mean centipedes!"

And then they all said, "We *know* you couldn't mean cockroaches!"

"The only thing I didn't mean," said Shoebag, "was a seven-legged, black jumping spider."

107

*　　*　　*

The world is very strange, Shoebag thought as he made his way down the hall after lunch. *I am strange.* We *all* are, for we cannot agree on who is all right and who is not. All we can do, it seems, is stick up for each other, and for ourselves.

"Stuella?" a lilting, teasing voice called out, "Time to stick up for Fatso! Time to get a sock in the face!"

Shoebag put his fists up as Mr. Biddle had taught him to.

When Tuffy Buck came charging at him, Shoebag did not duck back, but headed right toward him, as Mr. Biddle had instructed, and he used the secret move.

POW! POUGH! MRRRUMP!

Shoebag landed on the hard wooden floor in the school corridor.

Yes, the world is very strange, Shoebag thought. Not every lesson you learn in it helps, and you do not become a winner overnight.

"There's more where that came from!" Tuffy Buck called over his shoulder.

Shoebag was sure there was.

Seventeen

Mrs. Biddle was in her studio painting when Shoebag got home from school.

Quietly, in the dark kitchen, he took off his coat and put his bookbag on the kitchen chair.

"Mama?" he whispered. "Are you in here?"

"I'm right under the handle of the oven door, Son," she answered, "and I have bad news."

"Who did the jumping spider get this time?"

"No one, dear, but your father is not the same since Coffee Cup's death. He says we are going to move. We are going to catch the next Universal Parcel truck out of here!"

"But U.P. comes on Thursdays, Mama. That's only two days away!"

"He said he doesn't care if we end up in Alaska! He cannot bear to live here any longer, with memories of Coffee Cup on every ledge and in every crevice."

"What will happen to me, Mama?"

"You will have to live your life as a little person in the best way that you can."

"How can I do that with my family gone? I will worry myself sick about you!"

"His mind is made up," said Drainboard.

"Yes, my mind is made up!" Under The Toaster said. "Our roach neighbors from next door will be moving in here. They will be happy to get away from the fat, hairy, brown brother of the black jumping spider."

Shoebag turned around. His father's voice was coming from the calendar on the wall.

"What will I do without my family, Papa?"

"Kill the black jumping spider so the next family that moves in here will be able to make an arachnid-proof home for themselves. If you'd killed him before, we might still have little Coffee Cup with us."

"I am not that much of a person," Shoebag said sadly.

"I thought this was our home sweet home forever," said Drainboard. "I thought I'd see my oldest son grow up to be a big roach, too, but now that's all over."

"What if I do kill the black jumping spider? What if I get up the nerve to step on him?"

"It's too late now," said Under The Toaster.

"And you could never kill him, Son. We know that."

"I might! I'm going to try!"

"It's way too late," said Under The Toaster.

"Everytime I go up into the cupboard I see those coffee cups, and I remember my baby son when he was just a newborn nymph, crawling out of the scam of his egg case."

"What about your oldest son? What about me?" said Shoebag.

"You don't even look like a son of mine!" Under The Toaster complained.

"But here I am!" Shoebag was shouting.

Mrs. Biddle came out of her studio with a paint-brush in her hand. "Good!" she said. "I'm glad you're here. You have company upstairs waiting for you, Stuart Bagg."

Eighteen

Mildred paced back and forth between Shoebag and Gregor Samsa, as they sat in the darkened living room, with the sun sinking through the window in the twilight sky.

"I am sorry that I left school before you had the fight with Tuffy Buck," said Gregor Samsa. He was holding the little Watchman TV on his lap, stealing glances at it as he talked. "Pretty Soft won't come out, but she told me through the door of her bedroom about her accident, and that she saved the roach, and tried to kill the jumping spider."

"So you know now that she is not selfish or heartless," Shoebag said. "She has a black eye and black-and-blue marks to prove it."

"And her career is over," said Gregor. "That is the saddest part of that story. She is no longer a star."

Mildred had climbed up on Shoebag's lap. Her

teeth were chattering and she was drooling. Shoe-bag pushed her away.

"I hear you have a new club," Gregor Samsa said.

"It's just the rest of us. Do you want to join?"

"I'm not the unpopular type," he said, "except when I am back, when I am there, when I am In Bed. People scream at the very sight of me."

"That happens to the best of us," said Shoebag.

"It is what I hate most about that life."

"Not me," Shoebag said. "I would give anything to be my old self again."

Now Mildred was focusing her attention on Gregor, sitting by his leg, cuffing him with her paw, her jaws trembling.

Gregor said, "This cat picks up the traces of the old me. Cats are very clever animals, but soon she will leave my side, and go back to you."

"Mildred does as she pleases," said Shoebag. "You can't count on her to leave your side."

"She will," said Gregor, "as soon as I give you this."

He put down the Watchman long enough to take out a slip of paper. "Do you mean it when you say you wish you were yourself again?"

In Gregor's glasses, Shoebag could see his own antennae quivering with happiness at the very thought.

He told Gregor, "Oh, I do! I miss everything! I

even miss hiding, and I used to complain when I had to hide every time a light went on."

"I hate hiding!" said Gregor. "I like to be noticed!"

"I miss those old dark crevices, and I miss outwitting the Zap man," Shoebag said, "and now my family is moving away on the next U.P. truck. How I wish I could go with them!"

Gregor held the slip of paper in his hands. "I have been saving the secret formula written down here, thinking there might be another day when I would just as soon return to roachdom. But I know now I never will. If I want to be a star, I must concentrate all my energy on that. Look what happened to Pretty Soft when she let her attention stray to help you. You cannot have your mind in two places if you want to be a star!"

Gregor handed the slip of paper to Shoebag. The moment he did, Mildred moved away and sat at Shoebag's feet.

"Now I no longer have the power to go back, and to be there," said Gregor. "If you really, really mean that you would like to be your old self, this is what you must do."

Mildred began winding in and out of Shoebag's legs, hissing up at him.

Gregor said, "You wait until a Wednesday night. You go into a dark room by yourself. You take off all your clothes and shut your eyes. And then you say those words, written down on that paper. Don't look at the words yet, and don't say them until you are all ready."

Shoebag put the piece of paper in the pocket of his shirt. Then he reached up and turned on the table lamp, for it was dark outside now, and Gregor was speaking in a very mysterious tone.

"Anyone who says those words on a Wednesday night, in a dark room all alone, naked with closed eyes," said Gregor, "will be what he or she is meant to be."

Now Mildred was heading across the room, slowly, on tip-paw, stalking something that the lamplight had revealed.

"Are you *sure* this will really work?" Shoebag asked Gregor, who had gotten to his feet.

"Yes, it will really work, so long as you never share it with another. If you do that, it will lose its power for you, as it has for me now."

"What I don't see," said Shoebag, "is how you can turn your back on roachdom forever!"

Gregor Samsa stuck his Watchman in his pocket and took off his glasses to clean them across the front of his shirt.

"Even the light does not bother me anymore now, and I was a cockroach for a long, long time. I won't miss it at all."

"If the light doesn't bother you, maybe you would lend me those sunglasses until next Wednesday night," said Shoebag, who could see his shiny shell in them, and Gregor's human face.

"I'm sorry, but I need them, Shoebag. Meeting Pretty Soft gave me the idea to be a TV star. I am going to the studio tomorrow to see about it, so I have to look like a star!"

He put the glasses on again, and reached out to take Shoebag's hand and wish him luck.

Behind him, Mildred was crouched and staring at the table.

"Thank you for everything," Shoebag said. "You are a real person!"

"Yes, I *am* a real person for once and for all!" Gregor Samsa said.

Then, before he left the living room, he walked to where Mildred was watching the black jumping spider let itself down to the floor from a dragline off the table.

And Gregor Samsa did what any real person would do next. He put his foot down and squashed seven black legs and the thin silk attached, giving Shoebag a two-fingered farewell salute.

Nineteen

There was one glorious party late that night in the dark Biddle kitchen! Every cockroach within crawling distance was there to celebrate the death of the black, seven-legged jumping spider! Crumbs and grease and meat shreds were shared generously, and all the old roach songs were sung.

> *Hi de hi ho, we hunt high and low,*
> *In kitchens,*
> *Hey de hi ho, the parties we throw,*
> *In kitchens!*

No matter how vigorously Shoebag protested that he had not killed the spider, no one in his family believed him.

"You said you were going to try and do it, and you did!" Drainboard had told him. "We are so glad you did, Son, but we are also afraid of you now."

Under The Toaster had added, "You have become enough of a person to step on things, so stay away from this evening's celebration!"

"I have good news, though. . . ." But Shoebag could not get them to listen to him long enough to hear about the secret formula which would restore him to roachdom.

"From now on we are going to hide when we hear you coming," they had told him. "You can't blame us, can you?"

Right above the kitchen that night was another mood, and it was not one of celebration.

"Now this is the story," said Mr. Biddle as the family and Shoebag gathered in the living room. "Pretty Soft has been permanently replaced by Claudia Clapper, which means that we can no longer afford the services of Madam Grande de la Grande. Tomorrow, Pretty Soft will go to Beacon Hill Elementary School with Stuart Bagg."

"I cannot go anywhere with a face like this!" Pretty Soft cried out.

"I'll paint out your black eye," her mother said. "And I'll color your bruises with Peach Tone Acrylic Number Three. You'll look like anyone else."

"I won't feel like everyone else, though. I haven't had enough practice being a civilian."

"You have been a civilian most of your life," said Mr. Biddle, "and it is time to get back in touch with real people."

"I have to do it, too," said Mrs. Biddle. "I must stop painting and get a job."

"We must go on a very rigid new budget," said Mr. Biddle. "We are not going to touch one cent of Pretty Soft's college money. We have to save for the day Stuart Bagg goes to college, too."

"We must call Pretty Soft Eunice from now on," said Mrs. Biddle.

"I don't think I'll be going to college," Shoebag said.

"Of course you'll go to college!" said Mr. Biddle.

"Oh, yes, Stuart, you have to go to college," said Mrs. Biddle.

"I'm not going to college if you don't," Eunice told Shoebag.

"We are not going to take our summer vacation," said Mr. Biddle.

"The new microwave oven has to go back to the store," said Mrs. Biddle.

"This is not good news at all," said Shoebag.

"It is not that bad, either," said Mr. Biddle. "Now we are no different from any other family."

"We have definitely fallen on hard times," Eunice said.

Twenty

"If I were to go away," Shoebag asked Eunice while they walked down Beacon Hill to school, "would you miss me?"

"I have never played the part of anyone who misses someone," she answered. "But I know what it is like to miss being Pretty Soft. I miss her mirrors, and I miss learning her lines, and I'm going to miss all the money she made."

"Missing a person is different than missing your old self," Shoebag told her.

"I'd need a script and cue cards to know what that's like," she said. "I'd need to feel the heat from the cameras to know what that's like. Oh, Shoebag, don't remind me of the days when I was loved so much for doing so little."

"I won't," Shoebag said, "but just remember I'd miss you."

*   *   *

"This is my sister, Eunice Biddle," Shoebag told Mr. Doormatee.

And he said, "Pleased to meet you, Eunice. Remember that I am your principal, and there's a pal in principal."

Then Mr. Doormatee looked at her more closely and said, "Haven't I seen you on television? Aren't you the Pretty Soft girl?"

"I was once," said Eunice, "but now I am just another civilian."

She looked so forlorn that Shoebag hurried her down the hall. "Come and meet the rest of us," he said. "I want to introduce you to Fatso, The Ghost, Bark, Handles, and Two Times."

Everyone said, "Pleased to meet you," and Two Times said, "Pleased to meet you. Pleased to meet you. But you're Pretty Soft. Pretty Soft."

"I was once," said Eunice, "but now I'm like the rest of you."

It was a long, hard morning at Beacon Hill Elementary School. Madam Grande de la Grande had not tutored Eunice in geography, so when the teacher called on Eunice to name a river, Eunice said, "Old Man," since she had often heard Madam sing a song called "Old Man River."

"I am dumb, and I never knew it before," said Eunice to Shoebag, between classes.

"You're not dumb, you just haven't been told everything," Shoebag said.

During recess, when everyone played "catch" with a rubber ball, Eunice kept dropping it when it was thrown to her. Times she ran with it, she stumbled and scraped her knees, for she was not used to playing.

"I am clumsy, and I always thought I was graceful," said Eunice to Shoebag.

"Stop saying what you're not and say what you are," Shoebag said.

"What am I?"

"You're Pretty Soft," a familiar voice said. "You're a famous TV spokesgirl, and I would like your autograph."

There stood Tuffy Buck, wearing his father's red-and-black hunting cap, and a hunter's vest with many pockets. He put a piece of paper and a pencil in Eunice's hand.

She wrote: Formerly Pretty Soft.

"Formerly?" said Tuffy Buck. "If you were Pretty Soft formerly, who are you now?"

"Now," said Shoebag, "she's my sister."

"Why didn't you tell us you had a sister who was a TV star?" Tuffy Buck asked.

He did not wait for Shoebag's answer. He began to walk along beside Eunice and to ask her questions. What was it like to be a star? How much money did she make? What other stars did she meet?

When she answered Tuffy Buck's many ques-

122

tions, she began to sound like someone they both knew.

"My name was on every lip, Tuffy Buck, every lip!"

and

"I could not eat out anywhere, or shop, or sit in the sun, or play on the slides and the swings in the park."

and

"Oh, dear, oh, dear, it was dreadful how they loved me!"

Tuffy Buck listened with his eyes wide and his mouth hanging open.

When it was time for lunch, Tuffy Buck followed her through the cafeteria, offering to help carry her tray, do her homework, walk her home after school.

"I am the boss of the cloakroom, the recess yard, all the blocks that surround this school, Beacon Hill Park, and this cafeteria!" he told her. "Naturally you will want to eat at my table."

All through lunch, Shoebag thought of what he would miss when he was back with his shell safely over him, his wings at his side, his legs and cerci in place.

He would miss Fatso and The Ghost, Bark and Handles, and he would miss Two Times.

He sat with them at the front table, and played the game with them that he'd invented.

Here's to The Rest of Us,
Here's to the Best of Us,
Here's to us one and all!
Here's to, here's to, our power, our power,
Here's to lunch hour,
Here's to who's able,
To sit at this table!

. . . for now there were others in the Beacon Hill
Elementary School who pulled up chairs to join
them, shouting out lines and rhyming them. Ones
with big noses, and ones with little eyes, and ones
afraid of the dark, and ones who stuttered, and ones
who still wet their beds at night.

They could hear Eunice from all the way across
the cafeteria. "You have such good taste in clothes,
Tuffy Buck!"

"This is my father's hat. This is my father's vest.
Say congratulations to my father."

"I've never congratulated a single soul but myself," said Eunice, "because stars are the most
unselfish of people. They give of themselves tirelessly . . . and no one has more heart."

We pick up for each other,
We stick up for each other,
The rest of us know what to do!
What a, what a, crew, what a crew!

"And Stuart Bagg sticks up for *me!*" Fatso called
out at the end of another game.

Shoebag said, "But if I am ever gone, what will happen then?"

"The rest of us will handle it!" said Handles.

Shoebag smiled.

When Shoebag passed Mr. Doormatee in the hall, he said to him, "Thanks for being my pal," even though Shoebag could not think of any way the principal had ever been his pal.

"I'm a pal of those who need a pal," said Mr. Doormatee, squashing an ant under his shoe.

"Except that ant," Shoebag said.

"Ants don't belong in school, Stuart Bagg. I'm not a pal of those who don't belong in school. I'm a principal pal."

When Shoebag went to the cloakroom at two-thirty that afternoon, there was this note in his jacket pocket.

Just because I like your sister,
Do not get your hopes up, Mister,
You'll be hearing your own moans,
When I come to break your bones!

Shoebag would not miss the poems, or the boy who wrote them.

Late that night, when the house was very quiet, when no one in roachdom dared come out for fear that Shoebag would step on him, Shoebag opened the slip of paper with the secret formula written on it. After he memorized it, he went into the kitchen.

He did not turn on the light. He did take off all his clothes. He did close his eyes.

"Flit, flutter, quiver, quaver, totter, stagger, trumble, warble, wobble, wiggle, swing, and sway."

And then he heard his mother's voice call out, "Get your cerci moving! Hurry up, Shoebag!"

Shoebag moved his cerci.

He moved his two back legs.

He moved his two middle legs.

He moved his two front legs.

And his antennae.

"The cat from upstairs is two inches away from you, Shoebag!" cried Drainboard.

"I'm only half an inch away from you now," said Mildred, "and being out of a job has given me a ferocious appetite."

Twenty-one

The next morning there were two notes, side by side on the kitchen table.

From Stuart Bagg,
   Mr. and Mrs. Biddle: Thank you for everything. Do not worry about me for I have found my way home.

From Shoebag:
   Eunice: It is all right not to miss me. Good-bye is good-bye. If you ever want to remember me, though, save some crawling insect as you did the roach that night.

Mr. and Mrs. Biddle had overslept and were hurrying to finish breakfast and get on with their day.
   "We will miss Stuart Bagg," said Mr. Biddle, "but I am glad his amnesia is over. Now I must get to my store. The customers will be waiting."
   "And I must get to my first job interview of the

day," said Mrs. Biddle clearing away the dirty dishes from the table. "I will miss Stuart, too . . . Eunice? Why are you just sitting there. Get ready for school!"

"I can't believe he's gone," said Eunice.

"Honey, there are things to be done now, don't mope," said her father. "Get Mildred back upstairs. Ever since I came into this kitchen this morning, that cat's been crouched by the microwave. I think she's spent the night stalking something, maybe a spider or some other bug."

"The microwave!" said Mrs. Biddle. "I'm glad you reminded me. That has to be put in its box to go back to the store."

Eunice was staring at the note Shoebag had left, going over and over the words, as though they were lines she had to memorize.

Mr. Biddle said, "Shoo, Mildred!" as he got up and lifted the microwave into its box.

Mildred jumped from the counter to the table where Mr. Biddle placed the box.

"I'll just leave these dishes in the sink," said Mrs. Biddle. "I'm going to be late."

"I'll walk with you, dear," said Mr. Biddle. "We'll leave this box outside the door for Universal Parcel. . . . Don't be late for school, Eunice!"

Mildred tried to follow them, but Mr. Biddle lifted his shoe and pushed her back gently. "You go back upstairs!"

Then Eunice's parents were gone.

*   *   *

Eunice Biddle was surprised by the drop of moisture that fell from her eyes to her hand. Was she crying?

How could she be crying when there was no script to tell her to cry?

Mildred wound in and out of her legs, and ran to the door and back, trying to get Eunice to let her out, so she could sniff the box in the hall.

Another tear fell from Eunice's eyes.

This was not good. Her eyes would be red and swollen.

"He was very cute, Mildred," she said. "He was a nice little brother."

Mildred scratched on the door and mewed.

Then many tears came from her eyes, and Eunice went to get some Kleenex from the kitchen counter.

If she did not stop crying, she would be late for school.

There beside the toaster was her old mirror, and Eunice picked it up.

Would the old trick which she used to use when she was Pretty Soft work?

She held the mirror in her hands and looked at her reflection.

Then she could not remember the old words. All she could think to say were some words from Shoebag's note to her.

"It is all right not to miss me. Good-bye is good-bye."

129

Instead of the beautiful little girl named Pretty Soft, she saw a seven-year-old with a very red nose and teary eyes.

"Eunice Biddle," she said, and her reflection stuck out her tongue.

"Right you are!" it said. "Now get me to school. I have a lot of catching up to do."

Eunice Biddle laughed aloud and hurried to get her bookbag and her coat.

When she opened the door, Mildred ran past her legs into the hall and plunked herself down on top of the box.

"Sit there then," said Eunice, "but whatever it is you want inside that box, will soon be in the back of the U.P. truck."

So caught up with what was inside the box, Mildred did not even see a fat, hairy, brown eight-legged jumping spider arriving over the top of the door at the end of the hall. It let down its dragline, landing on the floor near Eunice's shoe.

"Moving in, are you?" said Eunice, and she was ready to step on it, when she remembered the rest of Shoebag's message.

Not only did she not grind it out with her shoe, but she carried it between two fingers, by the dragline, and put it safely inside the kitchen.

It was strange to walk down the hill to school without Shoebag. It was sad, too, but wherever

Shoebag was, Eunice knew he would miss her, because he had told her he would.

And she had remembered him, she thought, by saving that crawling insect in the hall. For Madam Grande de la Grande had never taught Eunice the difference between insects, which have six legs, and arachnids, which have eight.

By the time she got to the Beacon Hill Elementary school, neighboring roaches had moved into the Biddle apartment and were feasting on the toast crumbs, shocked when they heard the familiar arachnid voice of the other new arrival.

"INSECTS! YOUR DAYS ARE NUMBERED!"

Good-bye is good-bye, Eunice told herself, and she walked right by Tuffy Buck, who called out, "Pretty Soft? Pretty Soft? Wait!"

Eunice kept on going, frowning as the sun hit her eyes, grinning widely as she saw Bark, Handles, Two Times, Fatso, and The Ghost, running after them to play on the swings and the slides.

Twenty-two

W hat's that?"
  "A cat, that's all. A cat."
"Put the box in the back of the truck."
"Shoo, cat! Scat!"

Then for a long time, there were no human voices.
The box they were in was picked up and put down
many times. Shoebag had crawled out of the microwave and joined his family in the bottom of the
box.

It was a noisy, bumpy ride, full of stops and starts,
lasting many days, during which they fed on the
glue of the Super-Stik tape.

At last they arrived at their new home, a huge
store in a shopping center just outside Boston.

When they landed there, it was evening, almost
closing time.

They sneaked out into a section of the store called

Appliances, where they stayed up under a new refrigerator while Under The Toaster scouted for a permanent place.

All the television sets across the aisle were on.

"This doesn't look good to me," said Drainboard. "What will we eat here?"

"I saw some books in the next aisle," said Shoebag. "We can always eat the bindings."

"Ugh!" Drainboard's wings shuddered with distaste. "I've had my fill of sticky picnics. I hope this move isn't a mistake!"

A new tiny sister of Shoebag's hopped about nervously.

"Calm down, Frying Pan," Shoebag said gently. "Daddy will take care of everything."

"I don't want to live in Appliances," Radio said.

"We may have to find the toy department," said Drainboard. "Children always wander in eating, and we can live on their crumbs."

"There're too many people. We'll get stepped on!" said Wheaties Box.

"Sweethearts, there are no people around in a department store after nine at night. We'll have the run of the place."

"What if this store forbids you to eat and shop?" said Shoebag.

"Maybe it's not that fancy," Drainboard said.

For a while, the little cockroach family tried to nap, while Drainboard soothed them with an insect lullaby about the noble old order of Orthoptera, which they belonged to, along with grasshoppers and crickets.

A major order we are, sometimes with wings,
*   and sometimes not,*
Chewing mouthparts have we, as spiders,
*   ticks, and mites do not!*
Or-thop-tera are we! We crawl and fly
*   and . . .*

Shoebag wasn't paying attention. His mind was back on Beacon Hill.

He could not cry anymore, of course. Roaches never cried. But their memories were very good, which was how they found their way out of crevices and out from under things, into the darkness, for their picnics.

Shoebag was not thinking about the good old late night picnics, nor even about this new place filled with the sounds of shoppers and rock music coming from the record department.

Shoebag was thinking of his friend. He did not think of her as Eunice. Even though she was no longer a star, she would always be Pretty Soft in his mind. And he would always see her beauty. It would last forever. For even if she did not know how to miss him, he bet she would remember him.

Good-bye *is* good-bye. But friends remember friends.

*   *   *

Then, as Shoebag peeked out from under the refrigerator, he saw a familiar face.

It was on all the television sets lined up across from him. A dozen big pictures of Gregor Samsa.

"Does *your* smile smell?"

Where the mirrors used to be in his sunglasses, there were pictures of chewing gum packages.

"Chew Great Breath!" Gregor said with a grin.

Shoebag was so happy to see his other friend and his only real pal, he leaped off the defrost timer to the floor.

Just in time he escaped being crushed by a man's boot, and he ducked inside again.

"Good news! Good news!" he could hear Under The Toaster coming back from his search. "There's a deli department a floor away, with a dark closet right behind it!"

"Home sweet home," said Drainboard.

About the Author

Shoebag is a story about change, by a popular young-adult author who's changed her name, too, to Mary James.